Metaphorosis

April 2020

Beautifully made speculative fiction

Also from Metaphorosis

Metaphorosis

April 2020

edited by
B. Morris Allen

ISSN: 2573-136X (online)
ISBN: 978-1-64076-167-4 (e-book)
ISBN: 978-1-64076-168-1 (paperback)

Metaphorosis
a magazine of speculative fiction
from
Metaphorosis Publishing

Neskowin

April 2020

Revitalized

Jason P. Burnham

As she trudged down the alley, out of sight of the grey uniforms, Cenessa saw a small puddle.

But how?

Could it be a mirage? It was certainly hot enough. The dust she had stirred from the parched, cracked earth settled as she stood there, trying to figure out if she was hallucinating the water.

Behind her, the way was clear. In front of her, the puddle abutted the stone barrier at the dead end. Sandstone walls of the surrounding buildings rose high above. This was a back alley – no windows, no stairwells, and no machines to accidentally relinquish this precious fluid.

Where did it come from?

She stepped closer, curious to see if she was imagining it, nervous because someone was always watching. Any water you found legally belonged to the Resource Engagement Officers, but those with the power had written the laws...

No signs of monitoring equipment. If the REOs were watching, she could not identify their devices.

Maybe they don't know about it? Maybe it is too small for them to care about?

No, that could not be it. A memory of a bloody, exploding leg clawed at the inside of her skull. They had toyed with the thief, letting him run far enough to give him hope that he was getting away with it; escaping with less water than could fit into a coffee cup. The ensuing projectile, immaculately aimed, had obliterated his knee, tendon and sinew splattering the sand and imprinting on her retinas. But more than the mangled ligaments, the sight of wasted water rapidly evaporating haunted her. *Waterlarcene*, the REOs labeled him.

Their restriction was absolute, an insurmountable sequestration so long as the REOs remained in power...

So how did this puddle get here?

She preferred her knees without bullet holes and her organs on the inside, but it had been a long time since she had tasted anything other than cotton, urinated anything other than stinging piss, dark as clay.

Before they died, her parents had warned her about mirages and the other non-aqueous liquids she might encounter. The temptation to drink them would be so great, they said, she might not process the ramifications of drinking them until it was already too late.

Super-salt pools, acid baths, or simply pathogen-filled, putrid water. The REO sometimes left those alone if the counts were too high, but with scarcity comes ingenuity and the level of bacteria that could be cleared was increasing exponentially. Formerly deadly cesspools could now be repurposed to add to the REO's already excessive supply.

Which hazard is this?

She knelt by the liquid, checking the alley's entrance behind her and the walls for REO monitors again.

Is it worth the risk?

But the primitive parts of her hindbrain responsible for thirst regulation were screaming at her. *Drink! Just drink it!*

With great restraint, she briefly dipped a single finger into the puddle, yanking it out quickly to monitor for negative effects. There were none. Not immediately, at least – no burning, no tingling. She held it to her nose – no odor. Wet finger quivering, she plunged it back in, testing the depth. Her entire fingernail disappeared.

This is more fluid than I've had all week, she thought. After waiting long enough, she hoped, for any side effects of a non-aqueous liquid to have manifested, but not long enough to draw attention to her absence from the near-absolute reach of REO surveillance, she stooped further, her cracked lips burning as they touched the water. That was normal though. It always burned to drink.

Half the puddle was gone before she lifted her head. *Let's see them take this back.* Nausea rippled across her abdomen and into her throat, erupting in a belch.

Drink slower, she told herself. Did she dare risk the time to drink the rest? But finishing meant having strength to complete her trek. The ARC, the ironically antediluvian abbreviation for the Aquifer Reclamation Crusaders, had been whispering rumors about their impending attempt to take out the local REO at their headquarters. The rumor had been enough to prompt her journey. She would give anything to be there when the walls came down, opening the path to the forbidden fount she imagined inside. Sparkling, crystal blue water waiting for the crowd and her among it, surging forward with the collapse, guzzling the liquid ambrosia.

The cool comfort in her throat and the accompanying clear-headedness were irresistible.

She slurped up the rest of the water, the dusty silt in the last gulps barely registering as undesirable. It was not even the worst thing she had consumed this week.

What is this feeling? She stood above the dark spot in the dust, considering.

Refreshment.

Time would tell if it had been full of pathogens. If so, the diarrhea would dehydrate her more than she had been before she drank. That would almost certainly kill her.

But that would come later.

She exited the alley, shuffling her feet noticeably less than when she had entered.

Too noticeably.

She ran into the faded grey uniform before she saw them.

"You're looking awfully... hydrated, citizen."

They know.

Split lips were no excuse for her lack of speech this time.

"Where did you get the water?" asked the lead REO. But his visor was looking beyond her, at the...

At the dark spot. It was a setup. REO commissions for capturing waterlarcenes were real, as real as the water they had planted here. There was nowhere to run, nothing she could do to annul her consumption.

"What water?" The high caliber rifle bullet detonating the knee played on a loop in her head.

"Don't play ignorant. Our sensors can detect it on your breath. Your fractional expiration is too high. You drank water in the last," the REO looked at their visor's readout, "five minutes."

She shook her head and the REO responded in kind.

"Hard to forget that quickly."

Her muscles seized, frozen despite the midday sun, blocked in by the sandstone building to her rear and the huddle of REOs on her left and right.

When the butt of their rifle connected with her temple, Cenessa despaired, not for her life, but because she knew they would pump her stomach, stealing her water, stealing her chance to baptize herself in the REO's sequestered spring. Through the penumbra of coma, she strung together one last covetous thought.

How big will their water commission be if they bring in an entire failed ARC revolt?

See Jason P. Burnham's story "Revitalized" online at Metaphorosis.
If you liked it, leave a comment. Authors love that!
Remember to subscribe to our e-mail updates so you'll know when new stories are posted.

About the story

The inspiration for this story was climate anxiety and a general fear for our world and our species. Since

2016, the constant bombardment of daily desperation has worn on me. I worry constantly about what the future might be like for us and for our children, particularly the disadvantaged ones who will be the first to suffer the effects of progressive global catastrophe.

This story takes place in one possible future, wherein we have obliterated society as we know it. The Orwellian Big Brother exists (the Resource Engagement Officers), but their surveillance serves to identify and control clean water. This focus lines the pockets of their wealthy puppet masters. By keeping absolute control of clean water during a prolonged global drought, they keep all the cards, hold all the power. The REO doles out water to the plebeians as they see fit, also enforcing water larceny punishment with extreme malice. This, of course, is untenable to those underfoot. Revolutions have and will continue to occur, but are not successful. The story's desperate hopelessness finds its origins in this world.

One of the most unsettling parts of this future scenario is that it isn't that far off for many parts of our planet. Already marginalized groups face water and food scarcity on a daily basis. Most of us have never seen it, nor will, but it is there. Their voices are never heard. There could be a Cenessa out there right now being killed over a pittance of [insert life-sustaining resource here].

I hope that we can avoid this future and change our present so that the Cenessa's of the world never face the label *waterlarcene*.

A question for the author

Q: What book or books inspired you as a child?

A: Many, so many. In third grade, I had a reading award named after me by my elementary school teacher, Mrs. Charlene Joachim (RIP). I think I read something like 128 books that year. The next year, another kid SMASHED it with like 200 (?), but it was awesome to inspire others to read. Books that I haven't looked up and don't know if they stand the test of time, but still have warm memories of include:

The second book in the *Boxcar Children* series, *Surprise Island*. The kids were just out there, on their own, having a good time. The image/feeling I still remember from this book was independence and a sense of wonder, particularly with loft-style dwellings (oddly specific, I know).

Lots of people were probably inspired by *The Lion, the Witch, and the Wardrobe*, but *The Voyage of the Dawn Treader* sticks out to me the most. My memory is of them sailing through the ocean, seeing mysterious civilizations under the waters and the awe that came with reading that. Maybe the water was even made out of sugar? It was incredible. I know there's a lot of religious symbolism in those books, but I remember it for the wonderment at the worldbuilding.

The City of Gold and Lead by John Christopher: I actually read this second book in the *Tripods* trilogy first. It was a wild ride to drop in to, but I just remember the fascination of an adolescent being in a foreign place, discovering things. So cool.

Are you still a child in sixth grade? If so, I'll add *Sphere* by Michael Crichton, recommended by my teacher that year. Writing class with Ms. Imrie was when I first discovered people could actually write things. *Sphere* was a trip as a sixth-grader and the general aura of omniscient creepiness that I attribute to that book is why I think I like movies like those in the *Alien* franchise. I'm talking about the scenes before the peak action when everyone is starting to realize that they're in big trouble. Think the wheat scene in *Alien Covenant* when it's otherwise silent except the wind and they realize there are no animals **at all**.

For some reason, these four stand out the most. If you ask me next week, I might say *Encyclopedia Brown, Tales of the Bounty Hunters,* and *Jurassic Park*.

About the author

Jason P. Burnham (he/him) is an infectious diseases physician and researcher. He loves many things, among them sci-fi and speculative fiction, his wife, child, dog, metal music, Rancho Gordo beans, and equality (not necessarily in that order).

moparandgalen.wordpress.com, @AndGalen

Clod-Shodden

J.J. Drew

Part 1 – The Garden

There were many in the beginning, dozens of basil seedlings basking under the warm sky and nodding dreamily at one another as if to say, "you're growing, as am I, and that is right and good." They grew in groups of four, and their pot-mates, whose roots caressed their own, were especially dear to them, as dear as the sun and the summer breeze.

Then one day the Caretaker came much closer than usual. It stared down at a pot, plucked three of the young plants by the roots, and ate them. The lone remaining seedling watched in horror as its lifelong companions were crushed between enormous jaws and the scent of their juices tanged the humid blasts from the Caretaker's internal bellows. The Caretaker moved on to the next pot, where again all but one seedling was ripped from the mother soil, and these were dropped into a wicker basket, which slowly filled with small plants slumped on their sides, already starting to wilt as their exposed roots fruitlessly grasped for purchase. A pattern emerged. The news rustled down the rows.

"Only one is left in each pot."

"The largest and healthiest remain. All others die."

Each seedling surreptitiously checked itself for damage. Could it conceal that slightly wilted leaf? The small hole from an insect's nibble? Each stood as tall as possible, hoping to be the one chosen to survive, yet they were also ashamed at their own behavior, because survival meant condemning their pot-mates to die. And so, pot by pot, judgment was passed.

Finally, the massacre ended, and the corpses were carried away, but the Caretaker wasn't quite done. Before the survivors could process what had just happened, they were exiled to a distant land around the corner, the fabled "Frontyard". Their pots, the only homes they'd ever known, were stripped away, and they were transplanted into the ground, where probing roots could penetrate as deeply as they desired and never hit bottom, and each seedling silently swore that those roots would be directed downward more than outward from now on, for those who have had their loved ones ripped from their embrace ever hesitate to embrace anew.

The basil spent that night in shock, but as the sun rose the next morning, the seedlings began to whisper questions among themselves. Why? And what was next? Each sought answers from the others, but nobody had answers, so the questions whirled in circles until finally they settled upon their new neighbor, a gnarled old rosebush, who ignored them until the pressure of countless inquiries finally breached some internal threshold.

"Listen well, all of you, for I will only say this once. You have survived the culling, and there will not be another. Rest easy on that point. If you live cleanly and avoid bugs and rot, you will enjoy as full a life as any basil plant may hope for, so grow well until the summer's end."

"What happens after the summer?" one seedling asked.

The rose turned its attention to the speaker. It was the smallest of the bunch, a spindly little thing that had been selected not on its own merits but because its pot-mates had all been exceptionally small and frail. "Little Baldy, you don't know what you're asking. Are you sure you wish to hear the answer?"

Even as the puny plant nodded, the others began to chatter.

"Little Baldy!" they laughed.

"It's true! Be is little and be barely has any leaves." (Basil plants being hermaphroditic, they lack gendered pronouns and refer to each other as "that plant which is not myself, but is like myself in all ways that matter." As that's a bit of a mouthful, it's been translated here to "be/bim").

"All three of my pot-mates were larger than bim. It doesn't seem fair that be was selected and they weren't."

"Hey! That's right! How come be was chosen instead of one of my pot mates?"

As the chatter changed from amused to angry, only Little Baldy heeded the words of the Rose.

"For your kind, summer is all. There is no 'after.' "

Time passed and the plants grew. Little Baldy grew too, but be was partially shaded by larger neighbors. Their growth outpaced bis own, and what had once been a small difference in size became a significant one, leading to more shade, a more marked difference, and so on. Basking in the sun is, for a plant, something like meditation, a process that lets the plant lose itself in enjoyment and absorbs their full attention. Little Baldy, lacking the height to bask properly, turned bis attention to the world around them, which led to questions. Lots and lots and lots of questions.

The only one with answers was the rosebush.

The rose tried ignoring bim, then insulting bim, but Little Baldy persisted, and after several days they struck a deal.

The rose would answer three questions each day... only three, and only if Little Baldy refrained from asking further questions once the three were used up. Under this arrangement, Little Baldy learned the names of the animals and birds. Be learned that the creatures called "cars" weren't actually alive. Be learned that the rose was very old and had seen many generations of basil plants come and go.

Every evening, the voice of the Caretaker floated down from the window above them. At these times, the sound took on a distinctive cadence, different from the sounds it sometimes made around the plants. "What is the human saying?" Little Baldy asked one day.

"It's telling a story to the small humans."

"You already told me that yesterday. I meant what do the sounds mean? What's the story?"

The rose was amused. "You're getting smarter, asking questions with long answers. Very well, I'll try to translate."

Between a poor translation and a complete lack of context, the basil was baffled by the narrative itself, but be was intrigued by one of the creatures the story described.

"What is a 'fairy?' " be asked.

"Well, I've never seen one myself, but the stories say they have wings, so they must be some kind of bird. They can grant wishes, which, as far as I can tell, means they make things happen."

"What kind of things?"

"Just… things. Things that wouldn't happen normally, but that somebody wants very, very much. Oh, and they love plants."

"So if I wanted something very, very much, a fairy could help make it happen?"

"I guess so. But I don't think there are any around here. Why? Do you have a wish?"

"Yes. I'd like to be bigger."

"You don't need a fairy for that. You're growing every day."

"But only slowly. I'd like to be as tall as the other basil plants. Do you think a fairy could help me with that?"

The rose didn't answer for a long time, and when it did, it said only, "The agreement was three questions and I've already answered four."

The next morning, the Caretaker came outside very early and, to the basil plants' horror, it carried the wicker basket once again. "You lied!" Little Baldy yelled at the rose. "You said no more of us would die!"

"I spoke the truth. You won't die today," said the rose. "Sadly, though, this is goodbye, my bald little friend."

"Are you going to be killed?"

"No."

And then there was no further need to ask what was going to happen, because it began. One by one, the top of each plant was pinched off and tossed in the basket. A great soundless cry went up, but as each head was removed and another voice snuffed out, the volume steadily decreased. Little Baldy was near the end of the row, with ample time to see bis fate approach. Be cringed as bis neighbor's head was pinched off, and then... one of the small humans made noises from the window.

The Caretaker looked up from the plants to respond. The pair called back and forth a few times, and when the pruning resumed, the Caretaker moved directly to Little Baldy's other neighbor and continued to the end of the row.

When it was over, Little Baldy gazed in horror upon his maimed friends. "Are... are you all right?"

"Guuuuhhhh..." sap dribbled from fresh wounds.

"Clouddreamer? Fadeleaf? Bushytop? Please answer me! Somebasil! Anybasil!"

"They can't," the rose said gently. "Their minds are gone."

"What?!"

"I've never seen a basil plant escape the trimming before," the rose mused. "You're so small that the Caretaker must have thought you'd already been cut. I have to say, it'll be nice chatting with you for a few more weeks until you get the treatment."

"This will happen again?"

"Oh yes. They're not dead, after all. They'll grow back bigger and stronger than before, but they won't remember anything, not me, not you, not even themselves. They'll be like sprouts again. They'll give each other new names, and bask in the sun, and they'll be happy. At least, until the basket comes out again... and again... and again. And for them, every time will be the first time."

"You knew this was going to happen. Why didn't you warn them? Why didn't you warn ME? I thought you were my friend."

"What good is a warning? You'd have spent the past few weeks terrified instead of enjoying yourself. Look at your damaged friends. When they grow back, will you tell them? Will you have them spend their days dreading tomorrow? And when you join them in the next trimming, and your own memory is wiped clean, would you have me tell you of this day? Are you happier now, knowing what you know, than you were yesterday?"

"I... I don't know. I don't want to forget them, or you, and I certainly don't want to forget myself!"

"But you won't know you've forgotten," said the rose. "And look on the bright side. You wanted to be as tall as your neighbors, right? Looks like you got your wish."

The little plant wept tears of dew.

Over the next few days, the mutilated basil plants did indeed put forth new growth to replace what they had lost, and as they regained the ability to think, Little Baldy became an adult among infants. Be was given a new name, Genius, and when they had questions, be was the one they asked... but be avoided speaking of the past or the future.

Late one night, a strange creature appeared, one that even the rose had never seen before.

It was small, not much taller than the basil plants, and its movements were strange. It stood upright like the Caretaker, but instead of moving on two lanky limbs, it appeared to have no knees at all. It tipped its entire body from side to side as it swung itself along on two flat, pale feet.

"Excuse me!" Little Baldy called as it passed. "Could I ask you a question?"

The creature paused and turned one beady eye to the spindly youngster.

"I've never seen a plant move around like an animal before, and I was hoping you might tell me how you do it."

The eye blinked. "You think I'm a plant?"

"What else could you be? You certainly don't move like an animal, and you're shaped kind of like a stump, and you're blue and white like a flower, and your feet are the pale color of roots, and you even have leaves!"

"Leaves?" The creature's tone was like ice. "You think these..." it raised its two leaf-shaped limbs, "... are leaves?"

"Oh! I'm so sorry; I didn't mean to offend. Um... are they petals?"

"They're wings, you idiot! And I have a beak! Have you ever seen a plant with a beak?"

"No."

"So..." It lunged at Little Baldy, snapping the beak shut millimeters from bis tender leaves. "What am I?"

"A... bird?"

"And don't you forget it." The menacing beak was withdrawn with a self-satisfied air.

"But if you're a bird, why are you walking down the street? Wouldn't it be easier to fly?"

The bird stiffened, and Little Baldy had the dreadful feeling that be had said the wrong thing. However, the response came in an even tone. "It's too dark to fly at night."

"Oh."

"Ain't you a genius," the bird muttered as it resumed walking.

"Wait!"

"What?"

"How did you know my name? Can it be... are you... a fairy?"

The little basil plant suddenly became the subject of intense scrutiny. "What do you know of fairies?"

"I heard about them in a story. So you really are one?"

"A fairy penguin, yes."

"And can you truly grant wishes?"

"What?"

The words came in a rush. "That's why I asked how you move around. I wish to leave this place, only I don't know how. Can you help me? Please?"

The rose, who had, until now, observed in silence, spoke. "Remember, Little Baldy, your last wish didn't turn out to your liking. I'd advise caution."

"Caution?" the basil plant answered. "What good is caution? Caution means staying, and if I do that, I know exactly what my future holds. If this fairy can truly grant wishes, I'll take my chances." Be returned his attention to the fairy penguin. "So, can you help me?"

"Mmm, I don't know. Granting wishes is a lot of work. What's in it for me?"

"Well, I smell nice."

"And?"

"Um... I'm good company."

The rose stifled a laugh.

"And?"

"That's pretty much it."

"You know what?" said the penguin, "you've amused me. I think I will grant your wish, but in exchange you have to become my servant. You'll travel with me and do whatever I say. Deal?"

"Yes!"

"Ok." The penguin clacked its beak pensively. "Let's figure this out. I don't really know much about plants. What's keeping you from moving around right now?"

"My roots," Little Baldy answered simply. "They tie me to the earth, and if I pull them up, I can't eat or drink."

"Really? Let's see." The penguin grasped Little Baldy's stem and, with a great heave, ripped bim out of the ground."

"What are you doing!" cried the rose. "You'll kill bim!"

"Shut up and let me think." The penguin eyed the exposed roots critically. "You'll never be able to walk on those stringy little things. You'll just fall right over."

"I.... know..." Little Baldy gasped.

"So you need dirt to eat and feet to walk on. Seems to me like you can catch both those fish in one bite." It divided Little Baldy's roots into two parts and packed a wad of sticky mud around each half. Then it pulled the plant upright with its beak, stepped on each clump to flatten it out, and let go.

The basil plant swayed unsteadily, but didn't fall over.

"There you go! Feet and a meal all in one! See if you can walk on them."

The dirt shoes were heavy, but with a bit of experimentation Little Baldy worked out how to shift them forward, moving in an awkward shuffle that made the fairy penguin look downright graceful in comparison. By now every plant on the block was awake and observing, and laughter shimmied through the leaves, but Little Baldy didn't care. Be could move!

Be turned to the other basil plants. "You should all come, too! We'll find a new place to live, someplace safe from the Caretaker."

The responses came all at once.

"Safe? I haven't seen any danger."

"Are you allowed to move like that? I'm pretty sure that's not allowed."

"I don't want to get pulled up by the roots."

"Why would we want to leave?"

"Haha, you said 'leave'!"

"I like it here."

"The Caretaker is nice."

The penguin uttered a squealing croak, and everybody fell silent. "Oi, Genius, remember me? You're my servant now, and I have places to be, so let's go! Shake a leg! Err... so to speak."

Little Baldy cast one last, long look at his friends, then turned and followed the penguin down the starlit street.

Part 2 – The Ocean

That night was an overwhelming bombardment of firsts for Little Baldy. Being in motion made it feel as if the whole world was moving around bim. The silhouettes of the houses shifted constantly, strange angles sprouting and receding unpredictably. Things that looked small grew larger as they approached, and large things grew smaller behind them. Up and up and up they moved, for what seemed like an eternity, heading for the place where the sky met the road, but when they reached the top, the stars were suddenly far away again, and the world lay stretched before them, holding more streets and hills and houses than be'd ever imagined existed, and beyond them lay a vast smooth expanse the color of the night sky. It was so large that it took bim a moment to understand what be was seeing. Be gasped. "That's the biggest puddle I've ever seen!"

"A puddle? You dare call the mighty ocean a puddle?"

"Well, you don't have to get huffy about it. I haven't seen much of the world, and it looks like water to me."

"It is water."

"Oh." Be thought about this. "In that case, I'm confused."

The penguin pointed at a nearby oak. "What do you call that?"

"A tree."

"And are you a tree?"

Little Baldy laughed. "No, silly. I'm a basil plant!"

"But basil plants and trees are basically the same, right?"

"Oh no. Trees are much bigger and stronger than little plants like me could ever hope to be."

"Exactly."

"So... the ocean is a puddle tree?"

The penguin sighed. "Close enough."

It was daybreak by the time they reached the rocky shore, which was dotted with puddle-sized puddles called "tidepools."

The penguin carefully made its way out among these pools, snapping up anything that moved, while Little Baldy wobbled along behind and observed. Be was surprised to discover plants living in the pools. They were strange-looking with long tendrils instead of leaves, but they clung to the rocks as tightly as any land-plant gripped the ground. Be called out a greeting, but they didn't answer, only waving to bim from their world below the rippling surface with an alien, sinuous motion that seemed to beckon bim closer.

"If you fall in, you'll be dead before I can pull you out," said the penguin.

Little Baldy flinched backward, landing heavily on the heels of the dirt-clod shoes. How had be leaned out so far without noticing? "I... I'll just wait for you back there, ok?" Carefully avoiding the tidepools, be made his way back up the shore. Perhaps the hypnotic ocean-plants were more sinister than they appeared.

When the penguin had eaten its fill, it rejoined Little Baldy and they walked along the shore until they reached a place that was thick with greenery.

"Stand here and be quiet." The penguin nudged Little Baldy into the desired position at the edge of the greenery, then moved behind bim and began to scrape at the ground. "Your job is to make sure I stay in the shade. If the sun moves, you move to block it. You also need to stand guard. If you see any living creatures approach, tell me right away. Otherwise, don't say a word. Got it?"

"What are you going to do?" asked Little Baldy.

"Didn't I just say not to talk?"

"Oh. Sorry."

"Geez, you really are a genius, aren't you?"

"You know, I'm starting to think you don't mean that as a compliment."

"Shut up!"

Trembling, the basil plant fell silent.

"Better." The penguin settled into the shallow depression it had excavated. "I'm going to sleep. We'll move on at sundown."

Around noon, Little Baldy felt a dreadful tickling sensation. "Fairy! Hey Fairy!" he called.

The penguin jolted awake. "What is it?! A human? A dog? A hawk?"

"Here. On my stem. It's a grasshopper."

"You woke me up for that?!"

"It's a living creature, and you said..."

"I meant dangerous creatures. Not little bugs."

"Oh."

The penguin lay back down, but Little Baldy spoke again. "It's dangerous to me. Look, it's nibbling one of my leaves."

The penguin's beak flashed, and the grasshopper vanished down the spiked gullet. "Problem solved. Now I'm going back to sleep, and I don't want to be woken again unless there's something dangerous to me, understand?"

Little Baldy nodded.

That evening, the fairy penguin awoke to discover a half-dozen more grasshoppers had made themselves at home on the little basil plant, who was starting to look rather ragged around the edges. "Wow!" Do you always attract this many bugs?"

"I don't know. We didn't see them much back home."

The penguin cheerfully picked them off. "I figured you'd be useful, but I had no idea you'd attract food! This is great!"

"Great?!" Little Baldy shuddered. "Being infested is horrible!"

"C'mon, Genius, think! As long as we stick together, I get free meals, and you stay bug-free. It's perfect!"

"But they were on me half the day!"

The penguin looked bim over. "Doesn't look like they did too much damage, but you have a point. If there were a whole bunch at once... well... you're not very big. Tell you what, do you know how to count?"

"I can count to three. The rose taught me how."

"OK, then. Any time you get more than three bugs at once, you have permission to wake me up for a snack... err... to get cleaned off."

"But even one is just awful."

"Maybe I'm not making myself clear. Your choices are waking me when you get more than three, or not waking me at all. Now which will it be?"

"Three, please," Little Baldy said meekly.

And so began their long journey. At first
Little Baldy was constantly astonished by
the new things they saw, but as days
stretched into weeks, be began to see
patterns. One house looked much like
another, one garden much like another.
Domestic plants gawked. Wild plants
laughed. They traveled at night and rested
during the day, sometimes shifting a bit
inland, but always keeping the water on
their left and following the general path of
the shoreline. The constant change
became a stasis in its own right, and as
the days passed, Little Baldy's memories
all ran together. How long had they
traveled? How many times had summer
rainshowers come and gone? How many
days had be stood sentinel, enduring the
dreadful crawling of assorted insects,
counting one, two, three... one, two,
three... one, two, three... and perversely
hoping for a fourth so that be could
awaken the fairy and be cleansed? Be
could no longer recall, and those events
that stood out enough to imprint
themselves in bis memory were like shells
scattered on the sand, empty husks of

once-living memories with no anchor in time or place.

Late one night the fairy penguin was, as usual, waddling along the edges of tide pools, picking at the contents, when a sudden wave lifted it off its stony perch and sloshed it out to sea. Little Baldy cried out and rushed down to the waterline, but as be reached the edge of the tidepool, the penguin bobbed to the surface and, with an elegance of motion Little Baldy wouldn't have thought possible, zipped through the dark water and frantically clambered back onto the rocks.

"You can swim?"

The penguin shuddered away a spray of droplets. "When I must."

It was a warm afternoon and the dog had approached haphazardly, snuffling its way along the waterfront and occasionally eating bits of detritus or breaking into a sprint so that it could bite excitedly at the sand kicked up by its own passage. Little

Baldy whispered an alarm and the penguin was awake in an instant.

If they had remained still, perhaps the dog would have passed them by, for the tide had already washed away much of their trail, but the fairy penguin was too slow and clumsy to risk being caught in the open, and so it slipped away through the brush, while Little Baldy stayed put, comfortable in the knowledge that the dog would take no notice of one small plant among so many others.

Then the penguin, hidden somewhere in the brush, called to bim. "Hey, Genius! Come over here! Hurry!"

Little Baldy choked back bis urge to remain still and set out after the penguin, pressing through the dense brush with many a whispered "Pardon me," and a "did you see a blue and white bird pass this way?" The wild plants pointed bim to an abandoned rabbit hole where the penguin popped out, grabbed Little Baldy's clods in its beak, and yanked bim into the hole.

"Wait!" Little Baldy cried as bis clods thumped against the floor of the run and bis lower leaves were squashed uncomfortably against bis stem. "What are you doing!"

"I need you to plug the entrance!" the penguin hissed sotto-voce. "Now shush!"

But Little Baldy's rustling route through the bushes had attracted the dog's attention, and it heard the penguin speak. It was upon them in a flash, and when it saw that its prey was underground, it shoved its head into the hole, crushing Little Baldy against the edge of the tunnel.

Then it began to dig.

The burrow was deep, and the penguin easily retreated beyond the dog's reach, but Little Baldy was battered by the gouging claws for what felt like an eternity, until finally the dog found purchase underneath the dirt shoes and the small plant was scraped out of the hole and tossed clear.

The dog kept digging, and Little Baldy was showered with waves of sandy soil that at first stung bis wounds, then formed a comforting protective layer until the buildup grew heavier and heavier, and Little Baldy feared be would be crushed.

Finally everything grew still. An eternity passed, and Little Baldy made a wish. Be wished to see the sun and breathe fresh air just once more before be died.

The oppressive weight began to lift. and light returned to bis world. The penguin had come for bim.

"Are you dead?"

Too battered to speak, Little Baldy waved a leaf in confirmation of bis living status.

"Wow, that was pathetic." The penguin grabbed bis clods and pulled bim free of the remaining layer of soil. "I thought you'd at least be able to block a simple hole. Maybe if you had thorns..."

Despite bis lack of thorns, Little Baldy bristled. "Thorns? Thorns?! Look at me! I'm a mess! Two... no, three broken branches, and if I manage to keep half my leaves after this, I'll be amazed. You nearly got me killed!"

"Well excuse me for trying to save us some time. You're always bragging about how good you smell, aren't you? And dogs think with their noses, don't they? How hard would it have been to cover my scent?"

"I couldn't say, since you didn't shut up long enough to let it pass. It heard you. All we had to do was stay put. It would have gone away eventually."

"You think it's that easy?" yelled the penguin. "You think if you just sit quietly and wait long enough, your problems will all just go away? When you were buried just now, did sitting and waiting get you free? No. I had to dig you out, and you haven't even thanked me for my trouble!"

"I..."

"And what about back in that garden of yours? Would sitting and waiting have saved you from getting your top chopped? No! I had to step in and save you then, too! I clean the bugs off you, and I don't even like bugs that much! I show you how to travel safely, I help you and keep you alive, and what do you do for me in return? Nothing! You're completely useless! I don't know why I even bother. As a matter of fact, I don't think I will anymore. You're on your own." The penguin turned and waddled away.

"Wait!" cried Little Baldy. "You're right! You've saved my life twice now, and I've been nothing but selfish and ungrateful. Please, let me make it up to you. Let me stay with you long enough to repay you for everything you've done."

The penguin paused. "And how will you do that?"

"I don't really know just yet, but someday in the future, you may say to yourself 'Gee, a basil plant sure would be handy right about now,' and I want to be there when it happens. Please... let me stay with you."

"Fine. But I'd better not hear any more complaints."

"You won't. I promise."

Part 3 – The Cliffs

The days grew warmer and the rain less frequent. This was a mixed blessing for Little Baldy, as the clods grew firmer and lighter as they dried, making movement easier. However, at the penguin's recommendation, be spent most of that extra mobility making detours to puddles in well-watered gardens so that be could slake bis thirst.

The landscape slowly changed too, and the swathes of sand and flat stone dotted with tidepools gave way to rocky cliffs that rose steeply from the water and often forced the travelers inland in search of a navigable route.

As the landscape grew more jagged, the penguin's attitude began to change as well. It became more and more irritable, snapping at Little Baldy over the slightest thing until the basil fell almost completely silent rather than risk saying the wrong thing and sparking the little blue bird's wrath.

Then one gibbous-silver night, the penguin stopped and stared at a pair of tall cliffs with a small stretch of rocky beach nestled between them. They'd already passed a dozen similar stretches of shoreline, and to Little Baldy, this particular spot, while pretty, wasn't particularly remarkable. Yet the penguin's expression was one of horror, and its voice trembled as it said, "Genius?"

"Yes?" Little Baldy responded.

"Could you do me a favor?"

"Of course."

"See where the road curves up ahead? Could you walk up there and tell me what you see? I need to sit down for a moment."

Little Baldy scouted ahead and reported back. "It's the edge of a human town."

"Did you see an oddly-shaped house? One that looked like this?" With two swift flicks of the beak, the penguin drew a shape in the dirt.

"That's it! Have you been here before?"

The penguin nodded. "This is the beginning... and the end."

"I don't understand."

"I think it's time I told you about myself."

"In all the time we've traveled together, you never once asked me where I came from or where we were going. Why not?"

"We were going somewhere?"

"Of course. Why else would we have traveled so far?"

"I dunno. I just thought traveling was part of your nature, same as plants generally stay still."

To Little Baldy's astonishment, the penguin actually laughed. "No. I had a home once, and a family. Where I come from, there are lots and lots of little blue penguins like me. We slept in cozy burrows along the shore, and every evening we'd all swim out to sea to catch fish and play among the waves. Of course, there were larger animals that wanted to catch and eat us as much as we wanted to catch and eat fish, but they didn't show up all that often, and for the most part, life was good.

"Then, one particularly dark night, when a brewing storm blotted out the moonlight, an orca ambushed me. I've thought of that moment a thousand times, and I still can't figure out where it was hiding. The thing was massive, but I'd swear it popped up out of nowhere. I was in my prime then, young and strong and agile. I somehow managed to escape with my life, but by the time I finally shook it off, I was alone in unfamiliar waters... and that's when the storm broke.

"The waves turned into mountains. It took all my energy and focus just to stay afloat. For two nights and two days, the sky raged and the water crashed. On the third night, the world finally stilled, but I was hopelessly lost.

"A lot happened after that, but you really only need to know two things. One, I became terrified of swimming, and two, I eventually ended up here, looking at those exact cliffs you see before you now.

"I knew my family lived on the shore, so I decided to follow the water. I thought maybe, just maybe, if I only kept moving, I'd eventually find the place I once called home, or at least other fairy penguins. I haven't seen my own kind in such a terribly long time.

"And here we are, right back where I began. How long has it been? Three years? Four? I can't remember anymore, but I suppose it doesn't matter. Whatever land this is, I've walked its entire edge. There are no penguins here."

"There's you," Little Baldy pointed out.

"Yes. There's me." The penguin shut its eyes. "Just me."

Their journey stopped that night, and didn't resume. The penguin rarely spoke and spent its waking hours staring blankly at the ocean. Little Baldy found a comfortable spot at some distance from the bird, and settled in to watch over bis master, only approaching occasionally to offer meals of insects, which the bird ate mechanically, and this was the only food it consumed. It lost weight and blue feathers fell like leaves. Its once-shining coat turned patchy and dull.

The local plants were friendly and the seedlings particularly loved asking Little Baldy about bis travels. Basking in the sun, chatting with neighbors, and enjoying celebrity status, be quickly settled into a pleasant and peaceful rhythm. Yet the penguin's misery was contagious, and Little Baldy couldn't enjoy life without feeling guilty about that enjoyment.

One day, be timidly approached the bird. "It's been pretty dry lately, and a squirrel told me there's a garden on the other side of the pointy house. I'm gonna go look for a puddle to soak my clods. Do you want to come along?"

The penguin mutely shook its head and turned away, then sudden sat up and stared at the basil plant as if seeing it for the first time. "That's it!"

"What?"

"You gave me the solution the day we met! I can't believe I didn't think of it before! I may be afraid of swimming, but I'm a bird, aren't I? I have wings, don't I? Maybe I can fly across the ocean!"

"Wait... didn't you tell me that penguins can't fly?"

"Normally they don't, but normally plants don't walk either, and look at you! If a basil plant can travel cross country, I'm sure I can get airborne if I'm brave enough to try." It looked appraisingly at the shoreline. "You wanted to pay me back for saving you, right?"

"Y...yes."

"Well now's your chance. Follow me!" It marched down toward the little beach with Little Baldy right behind.

As they neared the water, it pointed up at the cliffs. "I'm going to climb up there and jump off. If I use the fall to build up speed, I bet I can catch some air and take off."

"That seems dangerous."

"It is. That's why you're going to sit down here and catch me if I fall. You're pretty bushy these days; you should be able to cushion the impact. If I fly, of course, I'll be leaving immediately, and you can consider your debt repaid.

An image welled up within Little Baldy's mind, broken branches and crushed leaves spattered with the penguin's blood. It seemed like a terrible idea... but be had promised to do anything, and with all the weight the penguin had lost, it might just be possible to actually break its fall without either of them getting too terribly injured. "I'm in."

"Positioning is everything," the penguin said conversationally as they edged along the bottom of the cliff. "There's a good overhang up there, so we just need to find the spot directly below it."

"Right here?" said Little Baldy.

"A bit to the side. Back. Now the other side. Back some more. OK, stay there for a minute."

As the penguin circled around to check the positioning from different angles, Little Baldy suddenly felt something cool on bis roots. A wave had edged over the rock where be stood and moistened the dry clods. Be trembled, afraid of being swept out to sea, but a moment later the wave receded, and the little plant relaxed. Be was safe and bis clods were well-moistened, which would save bim a trip to the garden! How convenient! Be stretched out bis roots and drank, but there was something strange about the water... something not right...

"I think be's coming around!"

Little Baldy felt as brittle and dry as last fall's leaves, but bis roots were immersed in cool, refreshing moisture and be drank greedily. As life trickled back into bis stem, be realized be was surrounded by towering plants, each twining up a rope to the wooden framework overhead. They smelled lovely and green, and were heavily laden with tomatoes.

"What happened? Where am I?"

The closest plant answered. "Dude, it was craaaazy! This freaky blue bird showed up out of nowhere, holding you in its beak. It dropped you in that puddle, packed some mud around your roots, spouted some nonsense, and then left.

"My... roots?" Little baldy was suddenly aware that bis roots felt strange. They'd been completely rearranged, and while these new clods were similar in size and shape to the one be'd used all summer, the composition of their soil was completely different. Be straightened up and looked around. The pointy house loomed nearby. This must be the garden the squirrel had mentioned. "What did the bird say?"

"Oh... Um... lemme think. It said not to let you drink any more stilt water..."

"Salt water," one of the other plants corrected.

"Right. Salt water... whatever that is. And then it said it would go atone to the drift."

"Do you mean 'go alone to the cliff'?!"

"No, I'm pretty sure it was 'atone to the drift.' And I remember the last part, because it rhymed. 'I'll fly or I'll die. Either way is goodbye.' Very poetic, don't you think?"

"No, no, no, no! I have to stop it! When did it leave?"

"Oh gosh, that was hours ago."

"To be honest, we were starting to think you were dead," its neighbor added conversationally.

Little Baldy waded out of the puddle, but the new clods were wet and sloppy and threatened to slide off at every step. There was no choice but to wait for them to dry out and firm up before moving further.

"Whoa! How'd you move like that?" asked the tomato.

Little Baldy wept.

The following afternoon, an observer would have seen a small basil plant hobbling along on feet of dirt to approach a patch of shore below a cliff. Little Baldy sat for a long time, scanning the rocks for some trace of the penguin, but there was nothing. Yesterday's footprints had been washed away by the tide, and if the fairy had fallen, the body had also washed away.

But Little Baldy hoped it hadn't fallen. Maybe, at the end, it really had managed to fly.

"I think," be said finally, "I'd like to go home too."

And so be turned and, for the first time, began traveling with the ocean on bis right.

Part 4 – Winter

Traveling alone was an entirely different experience from traveling with the penguin. Little Baldy got to decide everything. When to move. When to rest. Where to stop. Be experimented with traveling at different times of day and drifted much further inland than the penguin would ever have approved. It was tiring at times, being responsible for every little decision, but also tremendously freeing.

However, there were downsides as well. Be was lonely with nobody to talk to, and bugs were a constant nuisance. Be began resting in the most barren, open spaces be could find, places bugs generally shunned and where, if they did approach, they could be seen a long way off and avoided by moving away. But those places typically lacked water as well as the comforting presence of other plants to help block the wind, so that Little Baldy slowly grew woody and brittle.

Each day was shorter than the last, and while the sun shone as bright as ever, its warmth steadily diminished, until rain, once a cool welcome relief, became icy torture. Little Baldy wasn't really worried, though, until the trees began to drop their leaves, and the wild plants whispered that summer was over.

The rose's words, uttered a lifetime ago, echoed in bis mind.

For your kind, summer is all. There is no 'after.'

Bis destination was still many, many weeks of travel away, but Little Baldy pressed on. What else could be do?

Then one day, it snowed.

Weeping, Little Baldy took shelter under the silver green leaves and slender lavender flowers of a large sage bush.

"What's wrong, little one?" asked the sage.

"I'm trying to go home, but it's too far away. With this cold weather, I'll die before I get there. A rose once told me that 'for my kind, summer is all'. Now I understand what that meant."

"It's true that basil plants don't usually survive the winter, but you have a rather remarkable ability to move around. Why not hunker down someplace where summer never ends?"

"Even if such a place existed, sitting and waiting has never solved any of my problems."

"Really? I find it solves many of mine. This cold weather, for example. I've seen it many times before. If I wait long enough, eventually the world warms up and summer returns anew."

"I was buried alive once. Sitting and waiting would have gotten me killed."

"Ah, but your roots weren't damaged."

"How... how do you know that?"

"My dear little basil, as long as the root lives, leaves can always be replaced. Sitting and waiting would have taught you that, if you'd only given it a chance."

"But then, should I never have learned to walk in the first place? Was this all just a giant waste of time?"

"I wouldn't say that. Finding new ways to handle problems is never a bad thing. The trick is knowing when to move and when to stay still. For example, do you see that building over there?"

It was easy to see the one it meant. Made entirely of glass, lit on the inside, and full of plants, it glowed like a miniature sun made even brighter by the way its light sparkled off the falling snow.

"If I could move as you do, I'd go there. I think it may be exactly what you need."

"I'll give it a shot. Thanks."

As the basil plant shuffled off through the falling snow, the sage called after bim. "By the way, what's your name?"

"That's kind of a tricky question."

"Then give a tricky answer."

"Well, in my mind, I still call myself by the name I had as a seedling. 'Little Baldy,' even though I'm not little or bald anymore. My traveling companion, though, always called me by my other name, 'Genius.'"

"What a coincidence! That's my name, too!" said the sage.

"Really?"

"Indeed. But I'm keeping you out in the cold. Goodbye, my little name-twin, and good luck!"

Little Baldy had seen these human structures before, but had never bothered to investigate them, on the logic that having gone to such drastic lengths to escape one human, it was foolish to seek out others. But with the cold settling in, there was no time to be choosy.

Be approached the building, first nervously, then in wonderment at the warmth radiating from inside. But how to gain entry? The door was shut tight. With no way in, and nowhere to go, be hunkered down in the lee of the building and pressed against the glass to absorb what warmth it could offer. "Guess I'll try sitting and waiting," be murmured.

The following morning, a human crunched through the snow and opened the sliding door. While it tended the plants, Little Baldy slipped inside and hid behind some empty flower pots, giving bimself over to the ecstasy of warmth and humidity seeping back into half-frozen leaves and branches.

The inhabitants of the greenhouse had observed bim arrive, and after the human left, they bombarded bim with questions.

"How did you survive the cold?"

"Where did you come from?"

"What kind of plant are you?"

"Are you staying long?"

Little Baldy answered at length, and after the initial burst of curiosity was sated, it occurred to bim that there was one vital question nobody had asked, the one question be'd answered over and over throughout the summer. "Aren't you going to ask about how I move around?"

"Why? Is that unusual for your species?" asked a broad-leaved plant with flowers shaped like orange and yellow spiked mohawks.

"Very unusual! In all my travels, I've never met another moving plant."

"Really? How odd! All the mimosas over there can fold up their leaves in the most charming way, and see the venus flytraps in that corner? They move and eat bugs." It stretched a bit taller with pride. "We're all very exotic."

"Wow! Can you move, too?"

"Silly. I'm a bird-of-paradise! Who needs to move when you're as lovely as me? Humans take one look at my beautiful flowers and simply melt. And speaking of melting, it looks like you're dripping a bit. Why don't you find a nice pot and make yourself comfortable? There are plenty to spare. You can sit here by me!"

The pot it indicated was half-full of ancient, dried out potting soil. Little Baldy clambered up and was pleased to discover that the clods fit quite nicely inside. "A bird-of-paradise, you said? Are you a bird, then?"

"Oh no, Dear. That's just what I'm called. Because my flowers look like little birds." It flourished its blooms. "See? Now tell me more about this bird that looked like a flower!"

And as the plants, all so friendly and welcoming, leaned in to listen, Little Baldy thought to bimself, You may not be a bird... but I think this may indeed be Paradise.

The winter roared along outside, but the greenhouse was filled with warmth and laughter. The human seemed puzzled by the appearance of an extra plant, but cared for Little Baldy alongside the others. Little by little, the once-battered basil grew strong and lush. But as much as be enjoyed the physical care, it was the friendships be grew to truly treasure, especially with the bird-of-paradise, who had a kind word or gentle laugh for every occasion.

In all that time, though, Little Baldy was careful to keep bis roots within the confines of the clods. They curled around and wove tangled mats, never spreading to the soil underneath.

When the snow melted and the warmth of spring finally arrived, Little Baldy said bis goodbyes and slipped outside. Before setting out, though, be stopped by to visit the sage, who was delighted to see bim. "Is that really the same little basil I met so long ago? Look at all that growth. You look like a whole new plant!"

"Hi, Genius. I wanted to stop by and thank you for your help. You saved my life, you know. And the greenhouse, well... it's a wonderful place. Everybody there was kind and generous. They welcomed me into their home and made me feel like family."

"Then why do you sound so miserable?"

"Do I? I don't mean to. Now that it's springtime, I can finally go home."

"Why, that's great news! That's what you were trying to do when we first met, isn't it?"

"Yes."

"But you still don't sound happy."

"I already know it won't be like I remember. The basil plants I was raised with... well, they forgot about me long ago, and now that winter has come and gone, they're probably all dead, with a new generation of seedlings growing in their place. There's a rosebush I wouldn't mind seeing again, just to let it know I survived, but it was always kind of crabby and standoffish, and after an entire winter of such wonderful company... well, going back just doesn't sound that appealing anymore."

"Then why go at all?"

"I keep thinking about the new seedlings. Maybe I can convince them to come away with me before they get their tops chopped. I can show them that life doesn't have to be short and brutal. The summer is too short for me to bring them all the way back here, but I might be able to find another greenhouse that would take them in."

"I see. Truly a noble act."

Little Baldy sighed. "That's how it plays out in my mind, but I know they'll say 'no', just like my friends did. And if they did say 'yes', what would I do? I don't have the strength or the leverage to pull them up by the roots, and I don't know how to dig. And even if I did get them out of the ground, what then? The penguin who made these clods for me is long gone, and there are no other penguins to ask for help anywhere on our side of the ocean. I don't have the skills to make shoes for one seedling, let alone an entire row's worth. And it's so much harder to walk now! I didn't realize how much I'd grown until today. I'm so big and bushy I keep falling over. I tripped half a dozen times just coming here!"

"Don't take this the wrong way, but it sounds to me like you really don't want to go."

"I would if it weren't completely pointless! I can't save everybody. I can't save anybody. There's nothing for me there but heartache. But I swore I'd go home. I told everybody in the greenhouse I'd go home. I talked about it all winter. I'd look like a fool if I backed out now."

"Ah, well, you certainly wouldn't want to look foolish. After all, as we discussed at our last meeting, wisdom is knowing when to move, and when to stay still..."

"Exactly! Although now that I think about it... maybe it's better to look like a fool than to act like one."

"Could be."

That afternoon, when the human made its usual rounds of the greenhouse, it noticed the bird-of-paradise looked a bit droopy. Muttering about soil composition, the human began rummaging through some bins and attributed the rustling of leaves at its back to the light breeze entering through the open door. How surprised it would have been if it had turned around in that moment and seen a large basil plant waddle into the greenhouse and heave itself into a pot.

When the human had gone, the bird-of-paradise turned to its dear friend. "Why are you here? I thought you were going home?"

"I am home," said Little Baldy, and for the first time, be directed a root downward.

See J.J. Drew's story "Clod-Shodden" online at Metaphorosis.
If you liked it, leave a comment. Authors love that!

Remember to subscribe to our e-mail updates so you'll know when new stories are posted.

About the story

I was participating in a holiday story swap event, and my assigned prompt requested a story containing a sentient basil plant and an evil penguin.

The prompter probably expected something much sillier than what I delivered, but as I pondered basil gardening and how a sentient creature would react to such treatment, it struck me as less "silly" and more "existentially horrific." Thus "Clod-Shodden" was conceived.

A question for the author

Q: Have you always wanted to be a writer?

A: Honestly? No. I know there are many stories out there of people who started writing as children and completed their first novel draft in their teens.

That's not me.

While I've always loved reading, I never felt like I had stories to tell. Then, in my early thirties, a story idea popped into my head and refused to go away. I decided to write it down, if only to get it out of my mind.

I quickly discovered that my writing abilities weren't up to the task.

Determined to do the idea justice, I set about honing my craft, and the strangest thing happened. It was like a mental floodgate had opened; the more I wrote, the more ideas I had.

I've been writing ever since.

About the author

J.J. Drew lives in New Orleans where she spends her days writing, training animals, and singing.

Seven Scraps Unwritten

L. Chan

Scrap 1: Monograph on the four catechisms

The first catechism of Eulalia is DIVERSITY LEADS TO STRENGTH. Its sigil is a square made of four interlocked components, reminiscent of hands each grasping the wrist of the next, forming a box.

Scrap 1 has an annotation, handwritten: This logos is one of the most complex in the Logocracy of Eulalia. This and the other three logos are said to be without beginning, just as the Logocracy is without beginning. The scholarship of history needs to cut through this jingoism – even mountains have beginnings; so too our Logocracy. Any logos starts by erasing the parchment or substrate beneath it. What was erased to create Eulalia? To give way to the Logocracy?

Scrap 2: Transcript of the thesis defence of Thera

Thera: The Conceit in the Republic of Eulalia is not illusion, although most people think it is. The magic of Eulalia is delusion; instead of seeing things that aren't there, people believe things are there that are not. Consider the walls of the University. We do not need to paint them as other nations do; a trained logomancer needs only to scribe the logos for red upon them, and if enough people believe that the walls are red, everyone will.

Third chair: Apprentice Thera, you seek to ascend to Journeyer and you present the pap that we feed to children in school.

Thera: I present the converse, that the principle can be reversed. There is an antithesis to logomancy, and its roots are within what I just explained. What if the opposite could be achieved: that things could be uncreated, not by the delusion of the many but by the will of the few?

Seventh chair: A decade's worth of study, and you bring to us debunked theses, Journeyer. Your thesis defence need not proceed.

Thera: I am due my hour, honoured chair. The charter guarantees it, and I claim this right. We are unique amongst the kingdoms, alone in our system of rule, lasting as long as the other kingdoms but without strife and struggle. The same charter that keeps the peace and establishes the ten Chairs gives me an hour.

Seventh chair: Look how she demands. We should never have taken a mongrel 'mancer like you into the University. The Book of Lies is a myth; something for separatists and agitators and ingrates who do not value the gifts of Eulalia.

Thera: I did not mention the Book of Lies, honoured seventh.

Seventh chair: I'll not have you being smart-mouthed with a Chair, you backwoods child.

Tenth chair: Thera is my student, seventh. We are here to question her theories, not her lineage.

Seventh chair: No need to remind, Tenth; we would have known her as yours from her debasement of orthodoxy. Always abusing your discretion to bring us those furthest from the ways of the Logomancy. And encouraging them towards spurious inquiry.

Scrap 2 ends here. The full transcript has been forcefully torn out of University thesis records. Only this page survives. The scribe has no recollection of the exchange.

Scrap 3: 4th year Academic Report of Journeyer Thera

Journeyer Thera is but a middling student – a level belying her intellect. Her work, when she does apply herself, is brilliant. In her third year, she rather elegantly conjoined two obscure logos to solve a term problem at least a fifth more efficiently than the model answer. Had she handed in her solution on time, she would be in line for an academic prize and her choice of supervisors at the Academy.

In outlook, she is prone to distraction. She uses twice as much paper and ink as the next student, and most of it wasted on half scribbled proofs. Thera imbibes far too freely of the student presses, addled by dangerous thought when she isn't dashing her head out against ancient unsolved logos. A dreamer and not a completionist, and unlikely to go far in Logomancy.

I beseech you, honoured Proctor, not to accede to the Academy's assigned supervisor. She has done nothing to warrant being assigned a master of any note, let alone the Tenth Chair. Tell them that she is ill, that a tragedy has befallen her family. Were she to demonstrate her incompetence to the Tenth Chair, our department would be a laughing stock for years.

Scrap 4: Banned playbill circulated across the Academy campus

LIES LIES LIES LIES

THE LOGOCRACY IS NOT BUILT ON THE CATECHISMS. IT IS BUILT ON LIES. WHAT OF THE SHORTAGE, WHAT OF THE RIOTS, WHAT OF THE MASSACRES?

WHAT OF THE MISSING?

THE BOOK OF LIES IS REAL. THE BOOK OF LIES TAKES AWAY OUR HISTORY, OUR FRIENDS. THE FOUNDATIONS ARE

FALSE. THE CHAIRS ARE COMPLICIT. EVEN THE TENTH.

LIES LIES LIES

A scrawled message on the reverse:
   "Esteemed Tenth, the penmanship on the playbill is rather brutish; mayhap it has roots far from our fair capital? You grow nostalgic as your time wanes, sweet Tenth. Your protégé reminds me much of you in your youth. We value original thought, but within reasonable bounds: a lesson you have yet to teach young Thera. A warning from one chair to another, school young Thera quickly, lest the First chair withdraw your prerogative to choose your successor."

Scrap 5: The Rules of Succession of Eulalia, An Intercepted Dispatch from the H.E. Elevier, Emissary of the Empire Sound

The High Chair is rotated amongst the ten Chairs of the Logocracy, in the order of their numbers, each ruling a year in turn. Nine of the ten chairs have not changed since we started keeping records in Sound. They are immortal, but not like the Undying Queen of Dark Under The Mountain, who rules from her crystal sarcophagus. Some craft protects nine chairs, the easiest guess being logomancy, although the logos for immortality must then be a closely guarded secret. It would be of great import to the Emperor were we able to procure it.

Only the tenth chair changes. The means of succession are opaque. Once, at a formal dinner a month ago I asked the Fourth chair, a woman of startling plainness and skinnier than a broom handle, what purpose this served. She replied that hubris accretes to immortality like rust to old iron, and only the Tenth chair keeps them all honest. Influence could be brought to bear, if only we knew how they chose the Tenth. I sought the Tenth at the dinner, but could not procure an opportunity to speak with him; his evening was taken up by a young lady, broad shouldered and dark, from warmer climes. If there were reason for a simple student to be at a dinner thrown by the Logocracy, it is lost on me.

Nevertheless, elements of unrest also exist in Eulalia, albeit under control.

Insurgency could weaken Eulalia and be to our benefit, but Eulalia is frustratingly stable. More so than her neighbours with the same constraints of rain and crop, but absent the force of arms that would quell protest. Dissidents whisper of some branch of logomancy that we've not yet seen, something that erases instead of creates. Perhaps this is even more valuable than the secret of the nine chairs.

I have another minor complaint against our historians – the schooling provided to me about Eulilian history was far from accurate. For example, the reported riots amidst the famine two score years ago don't seem to have happened at all. The same with the attempted annexure of West Eulalia by our Empire seventy-six years ago. Nobody in the country remembers these, even amongst those with no love for the Logocracy. The further from home I get, the more ridiculous these histories sound. I tried to find them in the précis given to all Empire diplomats, but they seem to have gone. It appears the air itself in Eulalia cannot stomach lies like this.

Scrap 5 ends here. Elevier was known to have subsequently divorced his Empire wife, and settled down in the Eulalian capital for the rest of his life. He never left the city and continue to draw a modest but adequate pension from the Empire. He never communicated with his embassy again.

Scrap 6: Requisition chit for additional workmen for renovation works on the Academy Library

Name: Eksbrys, Sub-Chair of Library Management
To: Department of Works, Fourth Chair
Date: 21st Day of Winterterm
Order: 4 workmen from the Department of Conservation, to restore a partially collapsed wall in the library.

Scrap 6: Written on the overleaf of the chit, in the different writing. "As a sub-chair, you should have known to pay attention to works around the Folded Library. You know that the Book is inscribed on the walls within. Were it not for the quick actions of the Journeyer studying in the Folded Library, the men would have left with their memories intact, to great mischief. Still, a more permanent solution is needed. The Book must take care of them. You will see to pensions and compensation to their families – Second Chair."

Scrap 7: Excerpt from a graded assignment, submitted by Journeyer Athyl

Eulalian society is based on four simple rules; four catechisms each represented by a logos. The catechisms themselves are of breath-taking complexity; none but the most talented logomancers can even dream of scribing one, and their services are always in demand.

The craft of Logomancy turns towards the continued evolution of all our logos, the paring of superfluous lines, collapsing form until purer intent remains. Yet research on the four base logos of our society is forbidden by the ten chairs. Their forms remain archaic, with nested logos adding to needless intricacy.

That the ten chairs take such pains to develop the craft of Logomancy elsewhere, but forbid it on the catechisms is telling. That the law has been in place since the establishment of the positions of chairs suggests that the longevity of our means of government is linked to our catechisms. After all, our magic is based on delusion and what more powerful delusion is there than our belief in the catechisms?

So armed, I sought to dissect one of the logos representing the first catechism, and there it was – a subtle work, echoed in the other three catechisms: ancient sublogos speaking to life and regrowth, turned towards the continued rule of the chairs. In seeing the way out of one problem, I have found another. There is no reason why the magic could not go ten ways instead of nine.

While we remember the names of the tenth chairs through to the current, there has never been a death celebration for a single one. While not prone to the wilder theories circulating about the Academy campus, I cannot help but wonder at the potential for a double tragedy, that the tenth chair, with the opportunity to learn the secrets I've found here, has the opportunity to change the system and never does. Has the opportunity to grasp immortality but never does. Has the opportunity to die as the rest of us do, but is just another victim of the Book of Lies.

Scrap 7, Handwritten comments:

Dear Athyl, this is a promising start to your final year at the academy, but this paper should be rewritten in a less controversial manner, and perhaps one which less excoriates your thesis supervisor. You are right about more things than you know now, and headstrong, and hopeful. All the reasons why I chose you, all the reasons I was chosen.

The nine have hidden their power in the basic foundations of our country, but more terrifying is their power to erase, to make us forget. Even ascension is paid for by a tithe of memory, but we never forget hope. Even after they have unwritten what I was, I see in you what I hoped to be.

I invite you to join me in the library after hours. My name to the guards will see you in. Your craft has a ways to go before you can call yourself logomancer, but your mind can no longer be sharpened by the classroom. Your instruction will continue in the Folded Library, as mine once did.

Your Supervisor, Tenth Chair Thera.

*See L. Chan's story "Seven Scraps Unwritten"
online at Metaphorosis.
If you liked it, leave a comment. Authors love
that!
Remember to subscribe to our e-mail updates so
you'll know when new stories are posted.*

About the story

This story started out as an experiment in form –
namely epistolary or a list story, something I'd not
done before. It was tough going, managing world
building, plot, a message, and a magic system within
the word count. It started out with far less words,
which really didn't hit all the marks. I loved the
conceits of having open magic systems run on skill
and craft rather than on birthright, and how those
systems might be used to perpetuate systems of power
and abuse, and this story is the result.

A question for the author

Q: What's a genre you'd like to write, but don't or
can't?

A: I'd love to write a heist story, either cyberpunk or
fantasy. I've tried once or twice but the craft of getting
a good twist in plain sight, without resorting to pulling
stuff out of a hat has thus far eluded me. There's a lot
to love in the heist genre – getting a gang together,

often with new or old frictions, backstories, cool tricks and pulling things back from the brink at the last minute through redirection. One day, I'll get there.

About the author

L. Chan hails from Singapore. He spends most of his time wrangling two dogs. His work has appeared in places like *Translunar Travellers Lounge*, *Podcastle*, and *the Dark*. He tweets occasionally @lchanwrites.

lchanwrites.wordpress.com

Donald Q. Haute, Gentleman Inquisitator, and the Peril of the Pythogator

David A. Hewitt

Inquisitator's Log:
July 11, 20—; 11:53 pm
The Donald Q. Haute residence,
Springstump Township

The electromail came in the night, heralded by a *ping* from my desktop computing-box. My Inquisitator's training snapped me instantly from deepest REM to full wakefulness, and I leapt, puma-fashion, from the bed.

To: DQHInquisit8@squiggle.web
From: Ballyhoo495371475@orgom.net
Subject: Porthos lost! Please help!

A foreboding fell upon me. This *Porthos*: a priceless diamondjade idol of ancient Mesopocambria? A white-bearded guru-monk who'd discovered the Muddy Lotus of Immortality and been abducted by nefarious agents unknown? I opened the electromail with a lightning tap on my clickermouse.

Hi Mr. Qhoute,

Porthos disappeared yesterday. She was by the fence last I saw her, digging. She can squeeze under if she digs hard, but usually the afternoons are too humid, so she gives up to lie in the shade or lap up pool water. But this time when I came out she was gone.

Our yard borders on a grapefruit grove that borders on the Everglades. No sign of her in the grove, and the police WILL NOT HELP!!! No response from our flyers either.

I remembered you from an Internet about your investigations. I believe ONLY YOU can BRING PORTHOS BACK SAFE. I will of course cover part of your costs. Please reply ASAP!

Yours desperately,
Lusitania D. Ballyhoo
Philodendron Furlongs, FL

P.S. There are rumors of something prowling the Everglades nearby, a creature unknown to regular science.

P.S.S. Porthos is half malamute, one-quarter Himalayan yak terrier, and the other quarter is kind of a question mark.

Did I hesitate? Ha! A mysterious crypto-creature, coupled with a some-expenses-paid Florida wetlands vacation in the sunny summertime? I replied in a flash.

Will arrive in two days' time. Stop. Please prepare admixture of buckwheat flour and talcum powder, so I may begin immediately to dust for prints in the grove and in the Everglades beyond. Stop.

Yours in earnestness,
DQH

Inquisitator's Log:
July 13, 20—; 8:22 am
Springstump Municipal Aero-Jetplane Port

After a grueling day of preparation, I found myself at the aero-jetplane port, watching for my assistant. They'd paged her thrice: *Sammy Jo P—, please approach the ticket counter at Gate Zeta-*

Three-Dee. The aerocraft had boarded, and I was holding the gate, craning my neck, when finally she came jogging into view.

"What kept you?" I called.

"You said 9:30."

"No, 8:30; definitely 8:30. Did you mishear me?"

"Well, you said it only once, followed by a verbal list of, as I counted, twenty-seven items to buy... and didn't mention an airline or flight number, and hung up before I could get a word in edgewise—"

As the attendant herded us down the porta-tunnel, I admonished and exhorted my callow amanuensis.

"I've told you before, Sammy Jo: In the *Lexipaedia Inquisitatus* under E, you'll find neither hair nor hide of the word excuse. Don't you remember the Seventeenth Credo? *Excuses are like endocrine systems: everyone seems to have one, but there's no explaining what earthly purpose they serve.*"

We were buckling in when, under her breath, Sammy Jo mumbled what sounded like "funky Inquisitating can bind my adze." I presumed she was reciting—erringly—some obscure *Lexipaedia* entry.

Inquisitator's Log:
July 13, 20—; 2:42 pm
Philodendron Furlongs, South Florida

A handbill, evidently printed on a desktop computa-inker, adorned a telephone pole in front of the Ballyhoo residence:

LOST:
Answers to "Porthos"
Reward for Information Leading To

Above this was a digi-pic of the dear departed. His black-and-white eyes sparkled behind fluffs of black-and-white fur, right up to the tips of his scampish black-and-white ears. Black-and-white puffy legs terminated in perfectly proportioned black-and-white front paws.

"Colored ink might've done her more justice," said Sammy Jo.

Our tapping with the flamingo-themed doorknocker was answered by a respectable-looking platinum-haired EuroAmerican pensioner-gal wearing raccoon-themed slippers, shiny sweat-trousers, and a flamingo-themed hoodsweater. Love and grief, mingled with determination, burned behind black eyelashes as thick and vivacious as a lunging nest of newborn snakes.

She waved us in, and as she guided us to the kitchen table-ette, I introduced myself and Sammy Jo, "My assistant, protégée, and mentee."

"*Manatee??*" Ms. Ballyhoo blinked blankly. "So you're half—I mean, I didn't know that was possible..."

Sammy Jo explained, then—as an A.B.D. degree holder in the zoological sciences—the fine distinction between an apprentice and a cud-chewing aquatic mammal.

"Let's delay no longer!" I interjected. "Show me where your fur-bearing friend Porthos was last seen."

Our host led us onto a screened patio— *by Vesuvius, the humidity!!!*—where she pointed to a hole under the vinyl fence, beyond which loomed a grove of grapefruit trees. Turning back to Ms. Ballyhoo, I noted a wellspring of tears flooding her eyes; as my heartstrings twanged, I mentally genuflected to Madame Helena Rubinstein, inventor of waterproof mascara.

A professionally fenced grapefruit grove is no daunting target for the master Inquisitator, particularly when the gate boasts no lock, nor even a functioning latch. Yet dust as I might for paw-prints, or shoe-prints—I hadn't ruled out the vile crime of *caninus abductimem*—nothing was revealed, even by Sammy Jo's trained zoologist's eye or my ear-mounted maxi-magnifying lens. We *did* soon discern, though, that we were not alone in the grove.

"*We're not alone in the grove,*" whispered Sammy Jo.

My Inquisitator's keen fivefold senses told me she was right—and that this was no career grapefruitsman, this young fellow tramping toward us, yammering at his upraised porta-Y-Phone. A splash of bleached hair enmaned his pale, sparse-bearded face, and against the sun's ravages—*by Hephaestus's forges, the heat!!!*—he was warded only by a white Tee-shirt bearing the red MeeMeeMeeeToob® logo. As he approached he was filming his own face, which caused him to trip and tumble over a green grapefruit-to-be.

"He's one of those amateur Webnet journalists," I murmured. "*Log-floggers*, I believe they're called."

"Sounds about right," said Sammy Jo.

"Just what do you know," intoned the flogger, regaining his feet, "about the disappearance of Porthos, the Hound of the Ballyhoos?" He flipped the cam-phone upon us.

"First," said Sammy Jo, "a malamute-terrier cross is *not* a hound, you moth-wit. And second..." *Second* was a flurry of expletives and bleep-words I shan't repeat.

"Florida Statute X-slash-Zed-slash-Twenty-two, subsection Seven-Bee, proscribes filming private citizens without express signatory permission," I touchéd.

"Except," answered this gadfly, "when the subject is *in toto* of committing a crime... such as trespassing in a grapefruit grove."

He had us there. I sleeve-mopped my sweat-sopped brow.

"Um, *in toto*, Bumbledork?" said Sammy Jo. "Then there's how you've been filming *yourself* committing that same infraction..."

Undeterred, the fellow inched forward, cameraphone still rolling. I could now see his press-pass—*Largo Ponce* was his name—but a) it was clearly falsified, a home-rigged ID-card-and-lanyard mockup; and b) grapefruit groves do not, as a rule, rigorously verify press credentials.

I pointed pointedly. "That card might fool the rubes, but you've met your match-maker in this trained Inquisitator! Besides—a true journalist would carry a microphone adorned with teevee station initials."

At this, Ponce looked down to his sad excuse for a press-pass... and froze.

Beneath his Doo-Dee-Das sneakerkicks lay what appeared to be a shedded snake-skin—the largest this globe-roaming Inquisitator had ever seen. I'd read about the recent Everglades python infestoonment, so this was no great surprise. Then Sammy Jo gasped. She strode forward, and Largo Ponce the MeeMeeMeeeToober skipped back, clear of the skin-husk.

Sammy Jo gingerly hoisted the skin. Large. Thick. Then she spread it out, so it became clear to see...

The snake-skin sported a pair of what looked for all the world like short mesh sleeves. Whatever foul serpent had slouched toward the Ballyhoo house had *legs*.

We snooped around the grove further, seeking other traces of the *thing* whose cast-off husk we'd found. For Largo Ponce, the late-afternoon heat proved too much—as a native Floridian he was more acclimated to the bracing chill of airconditioned homes, airconditioned stores, airconditioned schools, and airconditioned automocars—so he soon departed.

The heat—*by Jove's thunderbolts, the heat!!!*—had begun to abate, and light was fading, as Sammy Jo and I scouted a last lip of turf abutting the Everglades.

"It's very wet," I observed.

"They call it the River of Grass," Sammy Jo replied.

"On a state map this region appears as land, but its actual state is hardly such stately dry land—aside from those little islands."

"Hammocks," said Sammy Jo.

"Ham-hocks? So called because they're frequented by the Everglades Ever-pig?"

"Ham-*mocks*," she repeated.

At that moment our conversationalizing, and the quiet of Everglades dusk, were interrupted by a swoosh-swooshing of boots in the long grass and the splish-splashing of... not far off, a scientific-looking bearded fellow, of pink-skinned Caucasian stock and middling age, was sampling with a scoop in the shallows at the Glades' edge. I hailed him.

"A fellow scientifico?" I called. He ignored me. The Inquisitator, though, is not lint on a trouser-leg, so easily brushed off. "Are you a student of the bio-ecologic disciplines?" Still nothing. I persisted: "What do you make, *monsignor*..." I motioned to Sammy Jo—who'd tucked the skin into her day-pack, and now produced it— "...of *this*?"

At the sight of what dangled from Sammy Jo's hands, he halted. Then he approached—a tall thick fellow in a very scientifically rigorous hat.

"Where... did you find this?"

"In the grove." Sammy Jo gestured. "The South Florida biome's outside my expertise, but still—something's *off* with this, isn't it?"

The bio-ecologist flusteredly unpocketed a tape-o'-the-measure and took the shedded skin's dimensions. He stared.

"So?" Sammy Jo gently refolded the skin.

"91 centimeters..." the eco-biologizer murmured. Then, assertively: "I'll need to take that for further study. This is federal parkland; you're not permitted to remove flora or fauna." He extended a hand.

"But what *is* it?" said Sammy Jo. "And who exactly are you?"

"Invasive species." The man *gimme*'d with his fingertips.

Sammy Jo looked to me. A *zoologist and her moult-leavings are not soon parted*, as the saying goes. But the Inquisitator's Code is clear about respecting authoritative personages. I scooped the skin from her reluctant hands and passed it to the man, along with my calling-card.

"Please contact me, sirrah, when you conclude anything. We're investigating a lost pet, who answers to *Porthos*, and fear this serpentonic invader may be implicated."

The fellow disregarded me, drifting away as one bedazed, gazing at the skin.

"You have to at least get his—" muttered Sammy Jo, then shouted, "What's your *name*?"

"Frank," the man answered, and departed into the Everglade night. Now a barking, distant but distinct, sounded over the waters. I marked my position, noted the time, and bi-angulated the sound's origin with the constellation Puppis. We'd no embarkable means of pursuing the barking this night; but pursue it we would.

Inquisitator's Log:
July 14, 20—; 6:24 am
Philodendron Furlongs, Florida

The flogger Largo Ponce came a-knocking early, as Sammy Jo and I were leaving the Ballyhoo home. We ignored him as we boarded the rent-a-mobile, until he crowed, "I got a *lot* of comments on that vlog—the most ever. Some da-bomb theories about Porthos, and about *it*. I even gave it a name."

Though Sammy Jo frowned fire, my training was to leave no stone's moss ungathered. "What theories, pray tell?"

"Well, like that old lady Ballyhoo kidnapped her own dog: a false-flag dognapping."

When I remo-unlocked the rent-a-mobile, Ponce yanked open a door and hurled himself into the back seat.

"You weren't invited," I scolded.

Sammy Jo shot a hand in and took hold of the young scamp's shoulder. "Why in shit's name would she kidnap her own dog?"

Ponce launched into an explication, holding up his 'phone to show a tangled chart of governmental and nonexistent-organizational connections. After three minutes, Sammy Jo muscled him from the automocar—he filmed this, of course.

"Maybe you're both actors in the false-flag too," he wailed. Sammy Jo started the rent-a, but before shutting my door, I turned to Ponce.

"You said you gave *it* a name?"

"I did. I call it... the *alli-thon*."

We'd found a purveyor of aeroprop-boats catering to early-rising swamp-hoppers. The sun was only just ascending behind us as, after a perfunctory tutorial, Sammy

Jo *brrrmmmm*'ed the aero-propulsor to a roar and blew us out into the vast shallows of the Everglades. Borrowing Sammy Jo's tech-a-phone, I web-skated to Ponce's flogsite: 7,204 views between dusk and dawn. Porthos's travails had set the flog-world afire.

I vigilated in the bow as we beelined toward the heading I'd marked. Alligators —the standard-issue type—drifted loggishly, while birds of every hue in the colored-pencil box fished, floated, or flapped all around. On one island—one hammock—after another, we disemboated and searched. But we heard no barking, nor saw sign of that other dread creature.

Inquisitator's Log:
July 14, 20—; 10:27 am
The Everglades, Florida

Hours later, dripping with sweat—*Deus Ex Infernus, the heat!!!*—and bebothered by buzz-bugs, we paused in a hammock-tree's shade. Sammy Jo tickled her Y-Phone's vidscreen.

"Oh … my … balls." Her eyes grew wide as sorcerers.

"What is it?"

"Largo Ponce..." She turned the 'phone my way. There was Ponce, wearing bespoke chest-waders, trudging knee-deep into the Everglades. He'd braved the heat and set off into this vastest of wetlands alone to find "*The Truth about Porthos!!!*" Some minutes in, he remarked that his batteries were "low as shit"—then gasped, spun the 'phone away from his own face... and it kept spinning and *ker-plupped* into the water. The vid-log murked, and blacked out.

"Oh ... my ... balls," Sammy Jo repeated.

The response was swift. By early afternoon the Everglades were humming with helichoppers, *brmm*'ing with aeroprop-boats, and hrumphing with hunters. We kept up our own search—for Porthos? For Ponce? In seeking we might find one, the other, or both, so seek we did.

As we aeroboated, we listened to floggers and major news channels alike speculating whether Ponce had merely mis-stepped, dropped his 'phone, and now wandered lost, or whether he'd been ensnared by... apparently none had watched the vidfootage where Ponce named the creature; they'd all taken to calling it the *croco-py*.

"In this vast queendom of *alligator mississippiensis*, *that's* what they call it?" Sammy Jo grumped as she cozied the boat up to yet another hammock. "Whatever it is, damn sure it's not a crocodile."

Every Y'all-Mart store south of Kissimmee must have been denuded of shot- and rifle- and autosemi-minicannon guns, of ammoshells, and of camocaps, camopants, camovests, and camototebags. A sporadic chorus of hues and cries; a popcorn-symphony of gunshots; the occasional *hissplash* of bullets hitting still waters. Hunters levelled their sights at gators, at imagined pythons—at anything that flitted, flapped, or skittered.

By early afternoon we spotted the first re-outfitted aeroprop-tour-boat, boasting a hand-painted sign:

CROCO-PY TOURS!! HELP FIND
PONCE AND PORTHOS!!!
ADULTS $23.00, CHILDREN $22.50

and at 2:12 pm, our august President lent the force of his bullying pull-pit by Tooting on his *Twit-horn* account:

Terrorist CROCO-PY strikes again and losercrats do nothing. Scumbags want IMMIGRANTS AND CROCO-PYS to eat your Real American babys. CrocOpy/Imigrant Wall... ...is only soLuTion.

Soon thereafter, more crackle of firearm-fire, then a distinctly proximate **THOOM**—and water poured in through a shotgun-spray bite in the 'boat's low-riding hull.

"*Swiftly!*" I cried. "*Give me your pants!*" Sammy Jo ignored me, though, preoccupied with something on her leg. Without a centi-second to waste, I yanked up my ankle-zippers, de-trousered myself, and stuffed my waterproof khaki M.M. Spleen breeches into the breach. This did prevent swampwater from swamping our boat; relieved, I turned to see Sammy Jo picking bloody slivers of aluminum boat-hull out of her lower leg. The wound was far from mortal, and as I applied second-aid, I mused upon what more dire danger we'd be in if *not* surrounded by good guys with guns.

Though uncertain of direction—Sammy Jo's Y-Phone lay now inert, devoided of charge—we carried on. Rampant as public response had been, we were at no moment alone. There were the two mustachioed AlabamaCaucasians—convinced Ponce and Porthos had been spirited away by a Bigfooted Sasquatch—who questioned us zealously. Then came the trio of bushy-bearded whitepeople Oregonians, certain these had been *Chupacabra* attacks—and that we were in cahoots with the *'cabra*. No sooner had we extricated ourselves from their Third Degree than a third group accosted us.

"Where are they?" accused the first of the quadrille of Michiganians, who also happened to be white, all dressed in flag-and-eagle-motifed jumpsuits. Who was I to judge apparelments, though, as with trousers stopping up boat leaks I greeted them in bare legs and Inquisitator-issue orange-drab undershorts?

"You mean Ponce and Porthos." Weariness weighted Sammy Jo's voice.

"*They know*," growled the second Michiganator.

"Wing fur," hissed the third, whose demeanor marked him as the squad *capitan*. "Search the boat. Search them."

"What do you urine-soaked shitstains think you're doing?!" protested Sammy Jo as the first two schlumped into our 'boat, tottering, splashing gladeswater over the gunwales.

"We've seen enough to know—" the leader eye-scoured us—"when somebody's in league with—"

"*Mothman*," singsonged the fourth, a short pinktanned fellow with eyes twitchy and wild as sparklers.

"Mothman?!" It was Sammy Jo's turn to bug her eyes out.

I intervened. "The Mothman, if such exists, is adapted to the monongahela silt loam and beech forests of west-southwestern West Virginia. Like a rare orchid or a hothouse zucchini, the likely-apocryphal Mothman could not readily inhabitate these sultry wetlands."

"Just what a fella'd say if he was hiding a Mothman," said the leader. One of his hench-hunters began to frisk Sammy Jo's dorsal area for concealed moth-wings; she beat his hands away.

A tense standoff ensued. These patriotic Americans were slinging guns, and I visualized which of my *Bart-itsu* moves might disarm multiple Mothmanites without overturning a watercraft. No sooner had I assumed a double-spearhand altercative pose, though, than the men relented and retreated to their own rent-a-vessel.

With a stridulous parting shot —"*Mothman lovers*"—the leader signaled the wiry fourth fellow to start the 'boat, which he did, repeating "*Mothman*" before throttling up and steering away.

As the afternoon wore on, Sammy Jo and I drew away, deeper into the River of Grass—away from the kerfuffular hullabaloo—and I confess we wound up adrift.

Refueling stations are not to be found on every block in the Everglades. In fact, there *are* no blocks in the Everglades. Thus we ended up, as Phoebus Apollo's punishing sun-chariot retreated to its nocturnal garage, stuck some yards away from a hammock—mucking through water to the waists of our chest-waders, tugging the dead-weight aeroprop-boat behind.

"I am gratified," I said, hands blistering on the tug-rope, "that we brought campage gear, in alignment with Inquisitator preparedness standards."

"A pup tent with no sleeping bags," groaned Sammy Jo. "And only because *I* added it to the list."

"Flint and tinder for fire—"

"A grill-lighter," she interrupted. "I knew which of us would spend a half-hour squatting in lacerating sawgrass, swiping with a rock for sparks."

"A packful of waterproof regulation playing cards, 52 plus jokers, to keep us diversionably entertained—"

"But not a drop of wine. Or beer. Or tequila. Or even gin," Sammy Jo finished. "Shows what you know about the great outdoors."

We'd arrived at the hammock. Sammy Jo tied off the 'boat, and we clambered onto land in the last vestiges of twilight. We moved toward what looked like open— if lumpy—ground beyond thick undergrowth, poking with a walking-stick to disperse any hostile fauna.

At the clearing's edge, under clouded moonlight, I handed my walking-stick to Sammy Jo and ignited my flash-torch as I moved to step onto the uneven ground. I halted, though, with foot poised in midair.

Much as *homo sapienses* have evening haunts, favored party-places, so apparently do alligators. The clearing where we'd intended to camp was one such nighttime hot-spot for saurians beyond count. And though they seemed unbothered by their own kin crowding against, slumping upon, even creeping over them, I intuited that my feet would elicit a different response—call it *speciesism*, but we weren't inclined to argue diversity theory with an alligator horde.

Treating absquatulation as the better part of valor, we turned tail.

From the refuge of the inert 'boat, we scanned the horizon. North-by-west-northwest, a wide tuft of growth broke the star-speckled horizon: another hammock.

Getting there, though, in an unmotile aeroprop-boat, was no easy matter. Harkening to Credo 71 of the Inquisitator's Code—*Be prepared; but if preparation is the parent, it's apparent that it must be paired with its providential progeny, improvisation*—we used a soup ladle and a metal meter-stick from our knapsacks as paddles to propel the heavy 'boat.

We were beyond weary when we heard the unmistakable *hummmm* of another aeroprop-boat.

Sammy Jo and I shouted and waved flashlights, and I even ignited a flare to brandish. The 'boat drew nearer... *rescuetour operator?... Everglades Five-Oh*

Swamppolice?... and then was upon us, droning down to a slow drift as the bow-wave rocked us. In the flare-glare, we saw the occupants: a teen-aged First Nations youth and his teen-aged girlfriend, half Indian and half—my keen Inquisitator's eye was hampered by harsh flare-light—Pakistani? Bengali? Indian?

"You guys okay?" the boy asked.

I bowed my gratitude. "For the moment, yes—"

"But we could use a ride, or a good splash of fuel, to get us back to civilization," Sammy Jo chimed in.

The boy shook his head. "I'm running on fumes. Pops has been draining the tank at nights—something about keeping me from running amok."

"We can send someone in the morning," the girl added. "We're not headed home just yet." Sammy Jo turned to me, rolled her eyes, and mouthed *teen-agers*.

Then she sighed. "I don't relish spending the night on the floor of this boat."

"Could you at least tow us to that hammock?" I gestured.

"Logni Isle? Not the best place to spend a night," the boy warned.

"Why not?" asked Sammy Jo, but both boy and girl merely shook their heads.

"We could tow you over there," said the boy. "But my advice would be to lay low, or better yet, don't get out of the boat."

They towed us—a slow progress, with their propellant-fan blowing hugely in our faces—and set us loose just offshore, promising again to send help in the morning. Then they rode off, with a mutual touching of gluteal regions—a form of contact I presumed must be rooted in Seminole or Miccosukee tradition.

"It's hot, even this time of night," I said. Sammy Jo and I lay curled discomfitedly in the 'boat, which we'd tied to an arching tree-root beside Logni Isle.

"Damn straight. And humid. And buggy. And sober."

"I suppose I ought to apologize. This was my Inquisition, yet here you are, ever-faithful Sammy Jo, bearing your part of the burden—including birdshot in the leg, no less—with admirable composure."

I heard her shift to face me. "What, you think I'm *surprised* to get into a bizarre and needlessly dangerous situation, accompanying you on one of these... whatever these trips are."

"Still," I answered. "Educating an aspiring Inquisitator is a delicate balance. As the *Lexipaedia Inquisitatus* points out, criticism comprises a conduit to consummate competency, while praise is potentially a poison. Sometimes, though, a compliment is warranted. You've been a worthy—"

Sammy Jo laughed, a musical sound. "As much as all this Inquisiting—"

"Inquisi*ta*ting," I corrected.

"—as all this Inquisi*ta*ting is kind of a... well, scientifically speaking, it's—you know..."

"Unconventional," I supplied.

She laughed again. "Unconventional. Right. Still, I've seen and done a lot I never would've, and it really is never a dull moment."

Sammy Jo inclined forward on the bench-slat between us. I sat up too. Our faces were close, in the murky-mooned night. Under her sweat- and rain-bedraggled mop of dark hair, those coffee-colored eyes were lovely.

"Have you," she half-whispered, "ever thought about—"

And just then a pattering rain began to fall, swiftly intensifying into a drumroll on the aluminum hull.

The quiet moment gave way to a flurry of action: pulling ponchos from packs, and endeavoring to cover the boat.

"We daren't sleep here," I said at last. Try as we might, rain could not be kept out; to slumber aboat was to risk swamping or drowning in the night.

So we set off with our supplies, with the tent, leaping onto wet roots for a foothold on the island. There we found a game-trail of sorts, about shoulder width. We followed its twists and turns, vaguely illumined by flashlight, in the pouring rain. The trail dead-ended at the best spot we'd seen, a flattish patch between the "knees" of a banyan tree. There we attempted to pitch our tent.

"Son of a bee-hutch!" Sammy Jo rasped.

I looked at her blankly.

"The tent fly—I took it out of my pack, digging for a poncho, and left it in the boat." With this, Sammy Jo tromped off, flashlight beam skimming before her. I sheltered as best I could in the fly-less tent, but rain poured right through the mesh crown and onto my own poncho-domed crown.

We'd pitched the tent facing the tree, so we'd have cover for any ingresses and egresses, and I'd left the zip-gap open in expectation of Sammy Jo's return. This proved to be an error when I heard a rustling from the entry behind me and felt the sudden shock of a tazerizer zapgunning my nervous system, rendering my finely honed neural reflexes useless. I then felt a net thrown over me, then a sack over my head, and a lariat-hoop pinned my arms to my torso. Visionless, I struggled, but more zapgunning broke my resistance, and I was dragged across a short span into what seemed, against all probability, to be an elevator.

Here I doubted my own sanity, but my razor-sharp Inquisitator's training kicked in and I sniffed. Yes—the distinctive scent of elevator was unmistakable.

What vile trap was this, yanking me from the safety of a rain-inundated, alligator-, insect-, and snake-inhabited hammock, down, down to some elevator-accessible Goblin-Town?

After some further dragging—I'd gone limp, to conserve my strength—the sack was pulled from my head. Blinking in fluorescing light, I saw a resoundingly luxuriant science-laboratory. The lab-table countertop was plated in gold, as were the faucet-taps. Plush velvet wallpaper descended to baseplates also trimmed in gold, which gave way to mahogany flooring, upon whose elegant hardwoodenness I now sprawled, bound. All around were cages or tanks housing mice, drosophila flies, geckos, garter snakes, and more.

And staring at me from my side was, to my shock and undoing, Dr. Frank.

"Why—" I began, then, curious, shifted gearshifters: "How do you afford all this?"

"I'm a global warming scientist," he answered. "So long as I propound the position of anthropogenic global warming, the government grants unlimited funding. Most global warming scientists have gold-plated laboratories and homes, while those who question human influence on climate live on dog food in hovels, at least until they're murdered by the black helicopters."

"You live here..." I posited. It is the Inquisitator's job to weld observation to intuition, forging a Sword of Knowingfulness that slices to the heart of things. The unmade bed in this studio-room, and the trash receptacle overflowing with micro-ovened meal containers were, I admit, useful clues.

He nodded. "Alone," he said, trying to hide a mournful note.

Yet this was not quite true: I glanced around again at the abundance of captivificated life. Then I gasped. In a large, well-appointed cage to my right, granite water and food bowls beside it bespeckled with what looked like diamonds, rested a familiar-looking specimen of *puppidoggus domesticus*.

"Porthos!"

Though she didn't rise, the wayward bitch twitched her ears, wagged her tail, and turned sleepy, soulful eyes my way.

"I found her again early this morning," said Dr. Frank. A thought struck him, and he patted himself for his keys, finding them at last in the pocket of his white silk lab coat. "But it wasn't her I was looking for."

Then it all became clear, clear as a solution of acetate blended with vodka. "The Croco-py!!!" I shouted. "It's the Croco-py, the Alli-thon, you were truly looking for!" Waving my leg at the test tubes, genesplicing machines, and enormous tank-enclosure at the room's center, I cried, "You are its creator! Its progenitator!"

He spun to face me. "Stop calling it that!! *Alli-thon?? Croco-py??!* Any culture that creates such idiotic mashed-up names..." Dr. Frank now began rummaging through drawers and cabinets full of science-doing thingamawhatzits, as I covertly struggled to free myself—without success. At last he found what he'd sought: a wire-y mesh of electro-nodes, which I surmised to be either a fiendish interrogation device or lights for a Christmas wreath.

But Christmas was five months away.

"Do you mean to torture me?"

Dr. Frank smiled. "I mean to wipe your memory. True, this will be its first test, but if the device works, all knowledge of me, my secret laboratory—and of the creature—will be erased. Forever."

"But the first two of those would be unnecessary if you'd simply not abducted me," I observed.

Dr. Frank scowled as he looked, next, for an extension cord. After further scrounging through drawers, cabinets, and piles he had just triumphantly produced an orange one, of the 50-foot variety—when the elevator bell *bing*'d.

Dr. Frank whirled, extension cord in one hand, tazerizer in the other, as Sammy Jo leapt through the 'vator door into the lab.

She was unarmed, nothing to hand but the aforementioned tent-fly. But seeing me bound on the floor, and a taser-armed scientificator glaring at her, Sammy Jo took action. Stretching the vinyl-plasticene tent-fly taut, she pump-twirled it from both ends, as middle-schoolers do to transform a wet towel into a rat's-tail bullywhip.

They circled one another like Florida panthers, if in fact enough of those still exist to ever encounter one another. A feint by one... a feint by the other... the crackle of a tazerizer; the crack of a tent-fly whip... the "Ouch!! That *stings*!!" of a bearded white man with a low pain threshold... then, in passing where I lay bound on the floor, Dr. Frank came too close.

I thrust out a leg and tripped him up, so that he stumbled; he dropped the tazerizer to break his fall. He recovered, but before he could recover the weapon, Sammy Jo covered the distance with a pounce like—I already used *panther*, so let's say a pounce like a caracal. As Dr.

Frank reached for the shock-gun, her fist shot out. It *thwumped* into his face. This time he sprawled onto the floor with an "*ow ow ow ow ow!!!*" while Sammy Jo also backed away, knuckle to mouth, squandering a layman's lifetime supply of *mother f-er*s and *son of a b-word*s.

"I've been doing kickboxing at the gym, but Jesus Christ a human face is fucking *hard!*" she shouted, and took it out on Dr. Frank by kicking him in the leg.

"Aaargh, Charley horse!" he wailed, and with this the outcome of the fisticuffs/footsicuffs was decided.

Sammy Jo commandeered the tazerizer and untied me while keeping a watchful eye on the now-very-mad scientist. We'd nearly reached the elevator when the bell *bing*'d one more time.

First Nations rescuers, whether teen-aged or otherwise? An accomplice of Dr. Frank's, to thwart our departure? A brown-uniformed National Park Service SWAT-battalion?

But when the doors opened, every one of us flinch-skittered back, for what emerged was—well, you've probably formed a mental picture already: half python, half alligator, enormous, though low to the floor and aero- and aqua-dynamic. Gliding into the lab, it eyed us all with a menace that transcended the reptilian and approached the human; we all recoiled still further. Yet it let us be, slither-plodding with surprising grace toward the chained Porthos. Though we dreaded what might come, not one of us deigned to intervene; instead we three, Sammy Jo, Dr. Frank, and I, all tumbled into the elevator and rammed fingers at the "UP" button.

The doors closed.

"You *created* that thing?" said Sammy Jo.

"I did." Dr. Frank's head slunk.

"But why?" I said.

"After decades of climate research, to strike fear into a populace that refuses to fear the more abstractly terrifying... to attempt what had never been done before... and maybe, just a little, because I wanted a companion..."

"You could've adopted a cat, or a dog," said Sammy Jo; the word *dog* sparked regrettable associations with poor Porthos. The elevator arrived at ground level and we all stepped out of the tree housing the elevator into a quiet night. The rain had stopped. Leaving the tent be —for lingering by the elevator was no option—we made our way over rain-saturated ground to where the airboat floated: our best refuge, though really no refuge at all. We sat silent in the boat, for minutes uncounted, until—

A rustling in the sawgrass.   We all sat bolt upright.

Sammy Jo pointed the beam of her flash-light. There, emerging from the sawgrass, was the face of the creature. Though its stare locked on us, it diverted course from our boat and slipped gracefully, soundlessly, into the water.

To our rejoicement, behind it came Porthos. The serpentuous creature cast a longing gaze that way, while Sammy Jo and I clapped our hands and called out:

"Porthos! Here girl! Come, Porthos!!"

Porthos vacillated, nosing at the creature, at us, back at the creature. Then we heard a voice we never expected to hear, a hissing, guttural, yet somehow mesmeric voice.

"*Come, Porthosss. The River of Grasss shall be bed, battthhhhh, and home to usss, and we will live in fffreedom, liberated fffrom hhhuman massstersss,*" spake the creature.

Fffreedom, though, is just another word for nothing left to lose; Porthos had waiting back at Ms. Ballyhoo's a cozy bed, frequent meals, and a sweater for when the Florida winters dipped below 68 degrees. Porthos made her choice: she hopped into the airboat, into the familiarity of human company.

And how is it that the creature, unholy amalgamism of the serpentastic and crocodillyicious, was able to speak in human tongues? Who can say? Genetic intermixing is ever a roll of the dice; the result here was fortuitous, allowing the creature to speak words thematically relevant to this tale.

Looking away from Porthos, to the sky, to stars behind thinning clouds, to cruel Fate, the creature crawled onto a nearby log of an icy pallor.

Dr. Frank called out: "Don't leave me! Stay! How can I bear knowing my child, my finest creation, is wandering alone, preying, wreaking destruction and inviting its own destruction too? Please…"

"*Sssuffering?*" the creature answered. "*What can you know of sssuffering? Of the sssuffering of a sssoul who, knowing right from wrong, virtue from vicccce, ssstill was forccced to track and kill the sssapient raccoon, the prissstine sssnowy egret, and the ffflamboyant ffflamingo, to sssate an unending hunger? The sssuffering of a sssensitive being who never got a sssingle sssyllable of reply from itsss brother the Burmessse pythhhon, or from the noble alligator, its sssissster?"*

"They don't really speak to *anyone*," Sammy Jo consoled; but the creature seemed not to hear.

"No companion, no love, no compassion, not even that of a fffaithhhful canine," it continued, stink-eyeing Porthos. The waters of the Everglades do flow, but at the glacial pace of about one meter per hour, so the log-bound creature had ample time to make its speech. In fact, I heard what sounded like claws paddling, an effort to speed things up. *"I shall keep drifffting until this log reachesss the extremity of the Earth'sss middle, letting hunger and the remorselesss sssun have their way, until I am extinguished entirely. What I have ssseen... I have ssseen murk of mud, rapture of rain, sssolaccce of sssky..."* The creature hissed more loudly, crescendoing toward a dramatic climax. *"I have ssseen shitheelsss burning rubber off the coassst of Pembroke Pinesss. All I've ssseen, all I've known, gone, like crocodile tearsss in the rain..."* It had drifted only inches, but the creature lowered its voice

to enhance the illusion of distance, so its final words carried but faintly over the water: "*The ressst isss sssilencccce.*" And it paddled harder and was borne away, very slowly, and was lost in the dank Florida dark.

Dr. Frank wept. Neither Sammy Jo nor I could muster any sympathy for him, though, and at length, to break the maudlin spell of his sobbing, Sammy Jo spoke up:

"It may have been derivative, but that was still far and away the most impressive fucking speech I have ever heard from a reptile."

At morning light, good as their word, the First Nations teens returned—and we were saved. Arriving at civilization, we parted ways with Dr. Frank, who'd sobbed and sniffled all night until even Porthos covered her ears. Sammy Jo suggested criminal charges. But Porthos had been well cared for; Florida has no statute against possession of an unlicensed python-alligator hybrid; my captivity had lasted mere minutes; and Dr. Frank had already tasted the business end of a

Sammy Jo drubbing. So we let bygones go on by, not least because even at 8 a.m., standing another minute out in the heat— *by Surtur's flaming Ragnarok-sword, the heat!!!*—was unthinkable.

Ms. Ballyhoo gushed at Porthos's homecoming, and produced the promised reward. And what of Largo Ponce? We heard no word, and in subsequent weeks, his webputer v-flog saw no postings.

Inquisitator's Log:
July 15, 20—; 5:43 pm
Bovard County Aero-Jetplane Port, Florida

"I said it before: Vloggers are *not* an endangered species," said Sammy Jo, as we sat in a Seattlebucks Coffee-café facing our departure gate.

"Keep in mind the 112th Maxim of the Inquisitator's Code: Every being is a manifestation of the All-nourishing UniForce, even a preening, mystifyingly self-absorbed log-flogger."

Sammy Jo pressed a napkin full of ice against her bruised knuckles. As for her enshrapnellated leg, our hostess had neatly antisepticized and bandaged it.

"Ms. Ballyhoo was definitely a manifestation of that. How much was the reward?"

"Let's just say that even after this coffee-and-pastry indulgence, enough will remain to pay the autocarpark fee back in fair Springstump Township."

Sammy Jo readied an ungenerous phrase, but I interrupted. "We must always recollect: Inquisition is its own reward. I'm just glad she and Porthos once again have one another. Companionship means so much to laypeople—those who have not chosen the solitudinous ways of the Inquisitator."

"Companionship," Sammy Jo repeated, and fixed me with a meaningful yet cryptic look. She raised her coffee mug. We clinked a toast. "Do you think that creature was right? That true companionship is a will-o-the-wisp, a flash of swamp-gas? That we're all, in the depths of our souls, truly alone? And also —are you going to eat the other half of that bearclaw?"

Her deeper questions had never been satisfactorily answered by scholar, poet, sage, nor even by the *Lexipaedia Inquisitatus*; as with the creature, only silence could be my answer.

I slid the plate across the table. With reflexes worthy of a true *Bart-itsu* adept, she snatched it up, and the bearclaw was soon borne away, and lost in the dark of Sammy Jo's gullet.

See David A. Hewitt's story "Donald Q. Haute, Gentleman Inquisitator, and the Peril of the Pythogator" online at Metaphorosis.
If you liked it, leave a comment. Authors love that!
Remember to subscribe to our e-mail updates so you'll know when new stories are posted.

About the story

Pinning down a story's origins is (for me, anyway) a dicey proposition. As best I can recall, this Donald Q. Haute story had multiple inspirations. This is actually my second story featuring Haute, who is of course a weird modern analogue to Don Quixote (with humblest apologies to the ghost of Cervantes for even pretending to attempt such a thing). A good friend works in South Florida as a marine biologist, and I once accompanied him on a sampling expedition in the coastal mangrove forests. Then there were the invasive pythons, which are apparently everywhere in the Everglades now, but which nobody seems able to find when they go looking. Then there was the social media three-thousand-ring circus that surrounds us all, and the impact that has on journalism, on facts, and on genuine connection with our fellow human beings. And then somehow Frankenstein's big, bad, grandiloquent creature and his latter-day Replicant offshoot crept into the mix as well. Plunk all these ingredients into a pot, let simmer for 3 - 14 months over low heat, stir well with revision and generous editorial aid, wait till timer says "BING!", and the result is "Donald Q. Haute, Gentleman Inquisitator, and the Peril of the Pythogator."

A question for the author

Q: What do you think makes a good story?

A: This is a profound question, by which I mean I find it virtually impossible to answer. If I could answer it conclusively, the number of rejection letters I receive would be much, much smaller. Sometimes it's the inventiveness or the beauty of the language that makes a story. Often it's that quality described by Jillsy Sloper in John Irving's *The World According to Garp*: "Most books you know nothin's gonna happen ... Other books ... you know just what's gonna happen, so you don't have to read them, either. But ... this book's so sick you know somethin's gonna happen, but you can't imagine what." Most often, that can't-look-away quality derives from the characters. They may be hard-boiled (Sam Spade, Easy Rawlins, Arya Stark); or perhaps they're soft-boiled (Huck Finn, Indiana Jones, Gabriel Conroy of Joyce's "The Dead"), or raw (Falstaff, George Eliot's Maggie Tulliver, The Incredible Hulk). In some cases they're even poached (Sanger Rainsford in "The Most Dangerous Game"). But some combination of compelling character and compelling need to see what comes next strikes me as being the closest thing to a magical formula for catching lightning in a bottle.

About the author

David Hewitt was born in Germany, grew up near Chicago, and lived for eight years in Japan, where he studied classical Japanese martial arts and grew up some more. A graduate of the University of Southern Maine's Stonecoast MFA program in Popular Fiction, he currently teaches English at the Community College of Baltimore County, but has at various times worked as a Japanese translator (specializing in anime), an instructor of martial arts, a cabinetmaker's assistant, a pizza/subs/beer delivery guy, and a pet shop boy. His hobbies include skiing, writing, meditation, writing, running, travel, and writing. His hobbies do not include jumping out of airplanes, rodeo riding, alligator wrangling, or deep-sea bathysphere exploration.

Copyright

Metaphorosis Publishing

Metaphorosis offers beautifully written science fiction and fantasy. Our imprints include:

Metaphorosis Magazine
plant based press
Metaphorosis Books
Driftwyrd
Vestige

Help keep Metaphorosis running at
Patreon.com/metaphorosis

See more about some of our books on the following pages.

Metaphorosis Magazine

Metaphorosis
a magazine of speculative fiction

Metaphorosis is an online speculative fiction magazine dedicated to quality writing. We publish an original story every week, along with author bios, interviews, and notes on story origins. Come and see us online at magazine.Metaphorosis.com

Keep Metaphorosis running! Support us at
Patreon.com/metaphorosis

You can also find us at:
Twitter: @MetaphorosisMag,
@MetaphorosisRev, @Metaphorosis
Facebook:
www.facebook.com/metaphorosis

We publish monthly print and e-book issues, as well as yearly Best of and Complete anthologies.

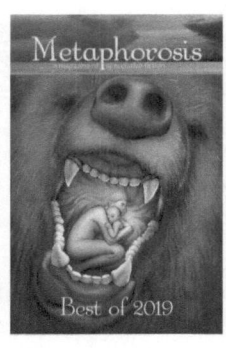 

Metaphorosis: Best of 2019

The best science fiction and fantasy stories from *Metaphorosis* magazine's fourth year.

Metaphorosis 2019

All the stories from *Metaphorosis* magazine's fourth year. Fifty-two great SFF stories.

Metaphorosis:
Best of 2018

The best science
fiction and fantasy
stories from
Metaphorosis
magazine's third
year.

Metaphorosis
2018

All the stories
from *Metaphorosis*
magazine's third
year. Fifty-two
great SFF stories.

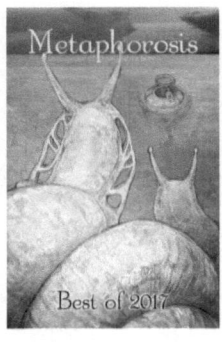 

Metaphorosis:
Best of 2017

The best science
fiction and fantasy
stories from
Metaphorosis
magazine's *second*
year.

Metaphorosis
2017

All the stories
from *Metaphorosis*
magazine's second
year. Fifty-three
great SFF stories.

Metaphorosis:
Best of 2016

The best science
fiction and fantasy
stories from
Metaphorosis
magazine's first
year.

Metaphorosis
2016

Almost all the
stories from
Metaphorosis
magazine's first
year.

Plant Based Press

plant
based
press

Vegan-friendly science fiction and fantasy, including an annual anthology of the year's best SFF stories.

Best Vegan SFF of 2019

The best vegan-friendly science fiction and fantasy stories of 2019!

Best Vegan SFF of 2018

The best vegan-friendly science fiction and fantasy stories of 2018!

Best Vegan SFF
of 2017

The best vegan-
friendly science
fiction and fantasy
stories of 2017!

Best Vegan SFF
of 2016

The best vegan-
friendly science
fiction and fantasy
stories of 2016!

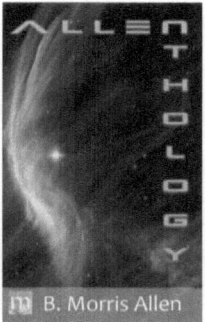

Susurrus

A darkly romantic story of magic, love, and suffering.

Allenthology: Volume I

A quarter century of SFF, including the full contents of the collections *Tocsin, Start with Stones,* and *Metaphorosis.*

Metaphorosis Books

Science fiction and fantasy books for writers – full of great stories, often with an additional focus on the craft of speculative fiction writing.

Score

an SFF symphony

What if stories were written like music? *Score* is an anthology of varied stories arranged to follow an emotional score from the heights of joy to the depths of despair – but always with a little hope shining through.

Reading 5X5

Five stories, five times

Twenty-five SFF authors, five base stories, five versions of each – see how different writers take on the same material, with stories in contemporary and high fantasy, soft and hard SF, and a mysterious 'other' category.

Reading 5X5

Writers' Edition

All the stories from the regular, readers' edition, plus two extra stories, the story seed, and authors' notes on writing. Over 100 pages of additional material specifically aimed at writers.